FORGOTTEN VOL. 1

My name is Kassey Cassedine Conwell. I am 15 years old and live in a foster home in the town of Baytonwood, Georgia. I've been from foster home to foster home since I was 4 years old. I don't really remember my parents that much and the passing years seem to make me forget more and more. The foster home I'm in now has one other child named Elisabeth. Elisabeth is two years younger than me. She's been here ever since she was a newborn. She doesn't know her parents at all. We haven't been really close since I've been here, but they told me I was leaving today and I've never been more upset about going to another home. This would be the sixth time I would have to leave.

I stand in my room, quickly packing up my clothes. I don't really own anything, so I only have enough to barely fill a bag. I have a few given pictures of my parents, notebooks, my phone, and some of my favorite foods that I stole from the kitchen. I got my phone from a foster dad I had in the past.

I closed my bag when I finished packing and slung it over my shoulder. When I walked out of my room, I looked around in the hallway. I heard voices coming from the kitchen. I slowly descended the stairs, sat near the top, and listened to the conversation.

"She's leaving soon and there isn't anything you can do about it." The voice sounded like the voice of an older woman.

"You can't take her! We were planning on adopting her sometime. It's not fair for her to keep jumping from home to home. She needs stability." The second voice sounded like my foster mother, Alice.

"Another family has asked for her and since you have signed nothing before they asked, we are taking her there. They have a bigger family, and I'm sure she will be happy." The first voice said.

I heard nothing else. There was a shuffling behind me, and I turned to see Lizzy. She stopped and glared at me with her arms crossed. "What are you doing?"

"None of your business." I answered casually and turned away from her.

"So, you're leaving today. I finally get the house to myself." She pressed.

"Great, Lizzie." I used the nickname she hates me using. It always unnerved her. I didn't have to turn to see her smile drop.

"Kassey?"

I jumped up and ran down the stairs. I was met with two women, Alice and my social worker, Ms. Reynolds. She was taller than Alice and was dressed like she was going to court. She had on a casual, all black suit and dress shoes. Her hair was tied back into a neat ponytail.

"Kassey, Ms. Reynolds will take you to your new foster home today." Alice explained to me. I looked at my foster mother. She didn't look happy about the arrangement, and from what I heard, she was totally against me leaving.

I didn't want to leave this house. I haven't been here long, but I liked Alice. Out of all the other homes I've been to, this was the best one by far.

Alice hugged me tightly. "I will always miss you being here. You felt like my daughter. I'm so sorry you have to move again. I was hoping I would be the home for you."

"It's alright, Alice. I enjoyed being here. You made things easy for me. I'll come visit sometime." I promised.

Alice smiled and kissed my cheek. Alice then stepped back and put her hands behind her back and put her head down. Ms. Reynolds turned to me with a face of almost no emotion.

"Follow me." She said, then walked out the door.

I moved to follow her, then paused in the doorway to look back. The room suddenly seemed smaller. I knew I would miss being here. I suddenly didn't want to leave, but I knew I had to. Gathering my courage, I stepped outside and closed the door behind me.

CHAPTER TWO

We sat in the car for hours without talking. It was ok with me. I could look out the window and think. I thought about the life I left behind and what was to come. I hoped the new family liked me. If not, I would have to move again.

I was so sick of going from home to home hoping to stay, only to have them crushed while I'm packing up my things. I stopped thinking that each home I went to would be permanent. I started telling myself that each place I went to was just an experiment. The only thing I had hoped for was me being able to find my parents. Once I turned 18, I was going to leave and go on my own to find them. I had always wondered where they were and if they thought about me sometimes. I had always wondered if they would send me postcards or come for me one day. I would sit by the window and watch the door, but nobody came.

We arrived at my new home. It was an enormous home that looked to be about two or three stories. There were two cars parked outside of two garages. They neatly cut the front lawn and gave off a scent of fresh grass. The time was Fall so there were leaves all spread out on the lawn as well. The house was white but faded brown in some places. I saw the mailbox read Johnson. We both got out of the car and walked towards the house. Ms. Reynolds rang the doorbell, and we waited.

I heard footsteps from somewhere inside the house. The door opened to reveal a middle-aged woman. She looked at us tiredly before her face lit up.

"You must be the social worker! Hi, I'm Hayley Johnson. Come in." She stepped back to let us both in.

It was warm inside the house. There were pictures on the walls, animal skins on the floors, and things hanging from the ceiling in other rooms. We walked into the living room as soon as we came into the house. We kept walking through the house and went to the kitchen, which was right next to the living room, only separated by a wall. The kitchen led to the backyard and had a door that looked like it led to a basement.

"We've been waiting for you. What's your name?" Hayley asked me.

I stared at her for a moment, deciding if I should answer. Ms. Reynolds shot me a glare, but I didn't flinch. She didn't know how much I wanted to go back to living with Alice.

"I'm Kassey." I mumbled.

"Well, Kassey, You are going to like it here. It's kind of crowded. There are four other kids, not including you. Two girls and two boys. I'm sure you'll get along." Hayley explained.

I nodded and left them as I went to observe the house. I held my bag tightly by my side. It was all I had of myself. All I had to show that I had lived because I owned nothing else. I found my way upstairs and trudged down the hall while looking into each room as I passed. I saw bunk beds, master beds, and twin beds. There didn't seem to be anyone here that was younger than 7 years old. I heard a noise behind me and I stopped. Slowly turning around, I looked to see a boy looking at me with a face of curiosity.

"You're the new kid, right?" His voice had a small, deep undertone. I figured he must be the oldest here.

I nodded. The boy was kinda cute. He was of medium height but still taller than my 5'2. He wore basic clothing: Blue pants and a watercolor shirt. His brown eyes surveyed my dark ones as he waited for me to say something.

"Well, we've been waiting for you to come. We all wanted to know what you were like. Hayley couldn't tell us. I'm Jason." He said while extending a hand.

I looked at it for a while before he lowered it. "You don't talk a lot, do you?"

I gave him a little smile. "Not really. They said nothing about me leaving until the day of."

"Well, do you want a tour?" Jason asked.

I nodded, and he took me around the house. It was bigger on the inside than the outside. There were 5 bedrooms, 4 bathrooms, a playroom, living room, kitchen, backyard, basement, garage, and a few open spaces with only carpet or wood. The place was a mansion. How did I get here? Why would anyone want to adopt or foster children if they lived here?

Jason stopped by my room. "No one has a roommate, so you'll be free to do whatever you want. Hayley doesn't hover, and we all like our privacy."

"Thanks." I walked into my room and looked around. It was kind of bare. There was a dresser that had a mirror attached. The bed was a twin size, with a wooden headboard. I leaned closer to see engravings of waves and birds on it. There was a little nightstand by my bed that had a black and white lamp on it. I shook my head and unpacked my things. Jason waited until I finished before suggesting that I meet the others.

*   *   *   *

Walking out to the backyard, I saw the younger kids playing, while the older kid was off to the side reading or on his phone. Jason and I walked outside, and the playing stopped. Everyone looked at us and I felt uneasy at all the attention. I didn't enjoy being stared at.

"Guys, this is Kassey. She just got here." Jason introduced me.

"Nice to meet you." One of the little girls said. I looked at her. She seemed to be the youngest.

"That's Aliyah, Cameron, and Jade. Aliyah is 7, Jade is 9, and Cameron is 16. We are going to be nice, right?" Jason asked them.

No one said anything. Aliyah ran to me and hugged my legs. I stood there, not knowing what to do. She smiled up at me.

"I'll be nice to you, Kassey." Aliyah said.

Jason laughed while looking at my face. "She's very passionate. Just a heads up."

"T-thanks..." I still didn't move. Aliyah seemed to sense my discomfort, and she backed up with a hurt expression.

"Dinner's ready!" Hayley appeared at the screen door. I could smell the aroma of food coming from the kitchen, and my stomach turned to knots. I didn't have an appetite to eat just yet.

Everyone went inside with me following them. They all sat in seats at the table and I chose the only empty one that was between Aliyah and Jason. Hayley brought out several dishes of food and placed them in front of us.

"Baked chicken and mack' n' cheese. You guy's favorite. Kassey, you like that, right?" Hayley asked suddenly.

Everyone turned to look at me. I cleared my throat. "I don't really eat meat."

They all looked at me, shocked. "Oh, well, what do you eat? I can make you something real quick." Hayley quickly suggested.

"Um, I don't really eat dinner. I'm fine."

"That's not good, Kassey." Jason said.

"Explains why you are so small." Cameron muttered.

Jason shot his brother a quick look, but he didn't notice. Hayley began serving everyone their food. "Are you sure you're not hungry? I can find you something." Jason asked as he got his food.

"I'm fine, Jason. I'm not hungry. Eating anything I normally wouldn't usually make me sick." I responded truthfully.

I couldn't remember a time when I ate dinner. All the homes I inhabited had diminished my appetite little by little until I ate like a mouse. I was quite contempt on the little bits of food I took for myself from time to time. Plus, eating more than I do now made me sick, so I preferred not to change my schedule.

"Kassey, tell us something about you. When were you born?" Hayley asked me.

"Um, I was born on February 20, 1997. I don't know where."

"February. Too bad that already passed." Aliyah said sadly.

"That doesn't mean we still can't do something." Jason said.

"I'm fine with nothing. Birthdays don't really mean anything to me." I shrugged.

"You are a very hard person to please." Cameron said, shaking his head. I raised an eyebrow.

"When were your parents born?" Jade asked.

"My dad was born November 19, 1973, and my mom was born on July 5, 1976." I answered offhandedly.

The rest of the dinner seemed to revolve around me, but I tried steering it in a different direction. I didn't enjoy talking about myself. It made me depressed because I didn't really have anything to talk about.

After dinner, Everyone cleaned up the kitchen. I tried to go my own way, but everyone, except Cameron and Jason, seemed to follow me. They asked me many questions and told me so many things that my head was spinning by the time I got to my room. I fell onto my bed and closed my eyes. Today was a very overwhelming day. I wasn't sure if I was happy about the change or not. I heard a knock on my door and saw Cameron standing in the doorway, looking at me with cautious eyes.

I sat up and beaconed for him to come in. Cameron walked slowly, as if he wasn't sure about why he was here. He stopped not very far from the door. There was a chair on my dresser and he took it.

"How are you liking your first day?" He asked softly.

I inhaled sharply. "Um, it was definitely something I won't forget."

He didn't seem to like my answer. "Why are you here?"

"What?"

"Didn't you have a home before this? Why didn't you stay there?"

His comment stung, but I didn't flinch. "I never had a stable home. They packed me up and took me here. It wasn't my choice."

"Well, tell them to take you back! This place is crowded enough without another kid coming in."

My blood boiled. "Who do you think you're talking to?" My hands started shaking.

"A child. We didn't ask for you to come here."

"Well, I didn't ask to be here either! It's not my fault they wanted to move me again! It's not your place to kick me out!" I screamed.

Jason's face appeared in the door. "I heard yelling. Everything ok?" He looked back and forth between me and Cameron.

"Yeah, we were just talking. I think we understand each other." Cameron smiled at me and left the room.

Jason looked at me. "Can I come in?"

I slowly nodded, and he sat in the same seat Cameron had taken. "What was that about?"

"He doesn't like me." I said bluntly.

"Cameron doesn't like anyone. What happened?" He searched my face, and I lowered my head so he couldn't read me.

"He told me I should've never come here, and that I wasn't welcome. That's basically what everyone says when I move. There's always one person who dislikes a new kid coming in." I spoke, seeing my past display in front of me.

"Well, Cam has no authority to kick you out. You're here to stay as long as Hayley wants. She already likes you." Jason tried to reassure me.

I said nothing. I knew this would happen, and it was part of the reason I didn't want to leave. I would never get to be adopted. I would never stop moving. It seemed that I would never have a home to stay in.

Jason hugged me and stepped out. I slid to the floor and crawled to a corner of the room. I curled up against the wall and tried to hide myself from the world.

CHAPTER THREE

The sunlight streamed through my open window the next morning. It blinded me as I opened my eyes and I spun away and groaned. Morning came too quickly.

I looked for my phone and saw that it was 11 in the morning. I was never an early riser, though it confused me as to why no one came to wake me. At Alice's, they always woke me before 10, even though I hated it. I then remembered that I was on the floor and that my face felt tight. I slowly stood up and walked to my dresser to look at myself in the mirror. My face was streaked with dry tears and my eyes were bigger than normal. I must have cried myself to sleep. Sighing, I went to find the bathroom.

The hallway was quiet, but I could hear voices downstairs. I found an empty bathroom and quickly worked to fix the disaster that was me. A few minutes later, I looked semi decent. My hair no longer had bedhead and my face was clean. I put my things back into the bag that I brought with me and opened the door to go back into my room. When I opened the door, I ran right into Cameron. I stumbled back and dropped my things onto the floor. I had to grip the edge of the sink to keep from falling as well. Cameron didn't seem shaken, just annoyed.

"What are you doing in here?" He asked sharply.

"Nothing, I was just leaving." I quickly gathered my things and walked past him. I didn't turn back. I just went into my room and quickly closed the door. I threw my bag onto the bed and sat down, panting. What was his problem? I haven't been here for 24 hours, and he already hated me. I knew I didn't have to put up with him and his aggressive behavior and I would not allow myself to. When I was sure I was breathing correctly, I got up and headed towards the door. I would have opened the door, but my hand stopped on the handle and my eyes looked at my dresser. I had put my parent's note in the drawer and I always read it when I woke up in the morning. It was one thing that helped to keep me sane. I walked towards the drawer, took out the note, and retreated to the bed. I stared at the wrinkled paper and the neatly written words. My mother wrote the note, but the words were from both of them. Besides the pictures, this was all I had left of them that was personal.

I took a deep breath and read it softly to myself like I've done many times before:

"Our dear daughter, we are so very sorry that we have to do this to you. If we could take you with us, you know we would. We did this to keep you safe. We hope you don't grow to resent us. It was the toughest decision we have ever had to make. It is not safe to bring you with us. We just hope you understand. We will come back to you someday. You are our little princess and you will never be far from our hearts. We will always love you.

Mom and Dad."

I didn't realize I was crying until I felt something run down my cheek. I quickly wiped the tears away with the back of my hand. The note never failed to make me emotional. I hated being emotional. I missed them so much, though I couldn't remember much about them. They would never be far from my heart. I would wait for them forever if I had to. I will find them one day. I had vowed that to myself when I was a child, and I vow that now. I gently folded the note and put it back inside the drawer. I took a deep breath and went downstairs.

I descended slowly. The voices grew louder and louder as I approached the kitchen. I saw Jason, Aliyah, and Hayley. I didn't see Jade or Cameron. I'm guessing that was a good thing. They heard me and all turned in my direction when I accidently stepped on a squeaky step. Aliyah was the first to smile and run towards me. I gave her a little smile and a pat on the back, which she happily took.

"You sleep a lot." She said.

"I didn't realize how late it was. I just woke up." I yawned.

"Are you hungry? We were just going to make something to eat for lunch." Hayley said.

"Lunch?" I asked. Was it really that late?

They all laughed. "You slept really late, Kassey." Jason said, chuckling.

I knew my face was flushed. "What were you going to make?" I walked up to the group.

"Well, I checked with your social worker, Ms. Reynolds, to see what you like to eat. She informed me that there weren't a lot of things that you preferred." Hayley said, sounding confused.

"I don't eat that much. I make my food most of the time and stay in my room." I confessed.

"You're a loner?" I heard another voice, and I turned to see Jade coming into the kitchen.

"Jade, that's not cool. She's not a loner." Jason said defensively.

"No, that's kinda true. I'm a bit of a loner." I tried to brighten up the mood.

They all smiled. "Can I talk to you for a bit?" Jason asked me.

I nodded, and he took me outside to the front yard. It still covered the ground in leaves of different colors and shapes. It was like a painting. None of it seemed real.

"I heard you crying last night. You alright?" Jason asked.

I stiffened. "Why would you think it was me?"

"I know the sound of everyone's crying here, even Hayley's. Yours is different. Plus, the walls are really thin." He said seriously.

I said nothing. I remembered little of anything that happened yesterday, only the argument I had with Cameron. After that, everything was a blur. I didn't know how to answer him, but he seemed to wait for me to say something.

"I think you heard something else. I don't know why you thought it was me." I lied.

He stared at me for a moment before saying, "You know you can trust me, right?"

I thought for a moment before nodding. "I think you and Aliyah are the easiest ones here to talk to."

"Thanks." A smile lit up his face.

The door opened and Hayley peeked her head out. "There was somewhere we were going to take you."

"Where?"

"It's a surprise. Hayley does it with every new kid who comes here. We all go to a different place every time so no one can spill it." Jason explained further.

"Everyone is getting ready to leave in a few minutes." Hayley said and went back into the house.

Jason turned back to me. "You alright?"

"Yeah, I'm good." *I need to learn how to get along with these kids if I want to stay here,* I thought. I couldn't keep arguing with Cameron or shying away from Aliyah. I needed to at least *try.* A few minutes later, everyone exited the house, and we began our walk.

Hayley had covered my eyes as we slowly approached the surprise. As soon as things started going dark, I panicked. Where were we going? What was happening? I tripped on pebbles and cracks in the road, and Jason held onto my arms to keep me steady. I didn't really care for surprises, but right now, my heart was thumping in my chest. We then stopped, and Hayley stepped away to clear my sight. As soon as I saw where we were, I felt overwhelming happiness. I stood there looking at an amusement park filled with obstacles and trees to hang from. It was empty, and we were the only ones there. I've always liked amusement parks since I was a kid. It was the only place where I could be wild and not be embarrassed by it. I took off running toward the vines that hung from the trees. I heard voices yelling behind me, but I ignored them. I grabbed the vine and pulled myself expertly up the tree. There was a small pond you were supposed to jump into when you let go. That was my favorite part.

I gathered my strength and swung myself back and forth until I was swinging high into the air. When I swung forward the last time, I let go and landed right in the water. The pond was deeper than it looked, but I knew how to swim. I got drenched, but I didn't care. I have never been happier than I am right now. When I came up, I got drowned with water as someone jumped in next to me. I wiped my face to see Jade resurface and spit water out. She had a grin that spread from one side of her face to the other.

"This is fun, huh?" Jade asked in a prominent voice.

"Yeah!" I laughed.

"This is the happiest we've ever seen you." Aliyah walked to the edge of the pond and looked at us. She sat down and dipped her feet into the water.

"I've always enjoyed being in or near the water. It's my favorite place." I explained.

"Can't imagine how water could make you *that* happy, especially considering where we've all come from." Aliyah muttered to herself, but I heard her.

"CANNONBALL!!!"

I looked up, a little too late, to see Jason's figure hurling towards us. There was a big splash, and we all went under. Jade came up gasping, and I came up laughing. I looked around for Jason and found him floating on his back. Aliyah screamed at us with complaints about getting her outfit drenched.

"What the hell was that?" Aliyah screamed.

"Such language." Jade said sarcastically.

"I have always wanted to do that and today was the best time to do so." Jason answered calmly.

"That was so unnecessary." I chimed in.

He opened one eye to look at me. "Says the one who ran like Satan was chasing her."

"Not the same thing." I argued, but a smile peeked through. I was so glad they had brought me here. I have been nowhere like this for a long time. I used to sneak out at night to go to a lake when I was little. Anytime that I was near the water, I felt like I was closer to my parents. I didn't know why. I just felt more secure and safe, more happy.

"Where's Cam?" Aliyah asked, as she looked around the park.

"I heard he was zip lining." Jade said.

"Zip lining?!" I asked. I definitely knew what I was going to do next.

Jason looked at me once and we both jumped up and splashed to the start of the pond. We got to the zipline, and we heard Cameron cheering as he zoomed past us. Jason whooped loudly to let him know we were watching him, and I laughed. We waited till he slowed down and got to the entrance of the ride. We helped to unbuckle him and he fell onto Jason as he tried to stand himself up. Cameron took one look at me and seemed as if he wanted to say something.

"We are going to have fun. No arguing, alright?" Jason said sternly as he looked at the two of us.

"I have nothing to argue about." I said quickly.

"Neither do I." Cameron agreed.

Jason nodded. He helped us all get situated with the zip lining equipment and then strapped himself in. Cameron taught us how to go forward, stop, and all the things we needed to know. I was in the front, so I was the first to go off. I sped off like lightning. The wind whipped at my hair and I put my arms out to touch the trees as I went by them. It felt great. I went higher and higher until everything below me looked tiny. I looked behind me to see Cameron and Jason catching up, but they were still pretty far away. The experience was exhilarating. It was dangerous, and it was the most fun I've had in a long time. I started slowing down and I willed myself to go faster.

"Kassey, look out!" A voice yelled.

I looked behind me and then looked back to be hit time after time with tree branches. I guess I wasn't paying enough attention to notice where I was going. I still didn't care. Bruises or not, I was still having fun and I would do this again in a heartbeat.

We all stopped at the end of the ride, and Jason worked to get us unbuckled. I felt dizzy as I landed on the ground and I fell over. Both boys ran to pick me up.

"You alright?" Cameron asked.

It surprised me that he wanted to know, but I didn't want to disturb the peace we suddenly had. "Yeah, I think I forgot to eat breakfast."

"Well, lunch and dinner too, but we'll eat when we get back. I think we have to leave, anyway." Jason said as he looked at something beyond me. Cameron and I turned to see Jade and Aliyah walking towards Hayley. When she caught our eyes, she waved at us. Our day out was over.

Everyone separated when we got back, but the excitement was still in the air. I still felt myself buzzing from the zip lining and jumping in the pond. It was the most fun I've had in a long time. When we got back, Jason made me eat something small so I wouldn't pass out.

"You already fell over once today. I don't want nothing else happening." He had said.

I sat in my room writing in my notebook on my bed. I've had my notebooks for as long as I could remember. I would write in them and then come back to them from time to time. They are kind of like a memento. I wanted to see if what I had felt before had changed. My notebooks were the only way I liked to express myself. It was private; it made me feel secure, and I wasn't exactly holding everything in. It was a healthy way for me to let go, a way I want to. The only two people who would listen would be me and the books. That was all I needed.

"It's becoming harder for me to express myself. I thought I was getting better, but they put me in another home and now I have to start all over again. It's been hard. I had a good day, though. Cameron was nice, and I did everything that I loved to do. I went zip lining, and I went swimming. I know I have to learn to get along with everyone here. I will …It will just take some time. I will try. For Mom and Dad. I know they would want me to have a family and that is what I will do. I don't want to move anymore. I want this to be where I stay. This will be the time for me to change my

future... for better... or for worse. I miss you guys. I hope we will see each other again soon...it's been hard to not have you guys in my life...I need you here with me."

I stopped writing before I could get emotional. I closed my book and put it beside me. Every moment I spent by myself was a moment that filled me with sadness and grief. I missed my parents so much; it was like a hole was in my chest. It hasn't healed in a long time and I have been looking for ways to help. Writing things down seemed to do little good.

"Kassey."

I jumped when I heard Cameron's voice. I didn't hear him come in and I didn't know how long he had been standing there. When I looked up, he was standing by the door with his hands in his pockets. He wasn't looking at me with a mean expression. His face didn't really show anything, at least nothing I could read. Cameron was as hard to read as I was.

"Can we talk?" He asked slowly.

"Yeah. You can sit down." I offered.

Cameron hesitated for a moment before sitting in the seat he took before. We stared at each other in silence for a moment. Neither of us knew what to do or say. I wanted to know why he suddenly wanted to talk and why he felt so uncomfortable. I would've started the conversation, but I didn't want to break whatever caused him to come in here.

"I know I've been a dick lately...I just didn't want another person coming here and changing things up again." Cameron started.

"Again?"

"When Aliyah came, she totally changed the routine around here. She was younger when she was here, so she needed more attention and that meant for more girls to be here than before... Hayley acts totally different around the girls. It—I just missed the days it was just me and Jason." Cameron explained.

I stared at him for a moment before I believed I understood. "You and Jason are close, huh?"

He took a moment to respond. "Yeah, we were. Now, he plays 'babysitter.'" He said bitterly.

"Cameron, I'm not trying to take Jason away from you. I barely wanted to be around a bunch of kids to begin with. I don't wish to change things between you two. I just want to stay somewhere I'm welcome." I said truthfully.

Cameron didn't answer, nor did he look at me. "If you want me to leave...then I'll tell Hayley that this will not work ou—"

Cameron's eyes flashed at me. "No! Look, I never meant to make an enemy out of you, ok? I just wanted to let you know I want nothing to change. Jason seems to like you and so do the others, so I guess I can learn to get along with you, too." Cameron gave me a half smile.

I smiled back. It felt good to be on his good side. We talked for a little while. He told me a little about everyone here and I told him what little I could about myself. We laughed and cried a little from laughing too hard. It was like we were actually siblings, like we had known each other forever. I didn't want this moment to end.

After Cameron left, I got myself ready for bed. I changed into my pajama clothes: a pair of black shorts and a white tank top. I got up and went to the mirror and put my hair in a ponytail. I've always had a small figure as long as I could remember. I didn't really eat a lot of meat and I often skipped meals, so my figure wasn't entirely healthy. I was in the middle of a struggle with my ponytail when I heard a knock on my door. I waved Jason in as I tried to finish what I was doing. He waited until I was finished before he spoke.

"I heard you and Cam had a heart to heart."

"Yeah, we did. He came in here and basically told me he didn't hate me. He just wanted to let me know where he stood and what he wanted and if I could accept that. I never wanted to fight with him."

"Cameron is a tough person to understand, but you kinda are, too, Kassey. You were going to clash, but when Cameron loves you, he does forever. He opens up to you completely. It's a thing with him. I'm just glad you're seeing that." Jason said happily.

"Well, I am too. I don't need an enemy here." I noticed his arms were behind his back. "What do you have there?"

"Oh, um, I brought you something." Jason walked up and showed me two little boxes. "Me, Hayley, Cameron, and the girls made and gave you things. A little welcome. Plus, Hayley was given this by someone named Alice." Jason explained as he gave me the boxes.

My heart skipped when I heard that name. Alice? The second box he gave me was the same box Alice gave me when I was living with her, and said it came from my parents. It had everything they wanted me to have. There was a note on the front that said, "I SAW THIS ON YOUR BED. IT'S

I thanked Jason and sat down with my new things. I opened the box of gifts first. I wanted to save the one from Alice and my parents. I wanted to enjoy it. The first box had food, cards, and little trinkets. Aliyah made me a few cards and pictures with me and her holding hands. Her cards were very colorful and very cute. I had to remember to thank her the next chance I got. Jade gave me pictures of her and Aliyah together. She also gave me a locket with a note attached that said, **"I HOPE YOU LIKE THIS. IT USED TO BE MINE, BUT I THOUGHT YOU WOULD LIKE IT. I CAN'T WAIT FOR US TO BE SISTERS. I HOPE YOU LIKE ME. I DON'T KNOW YOUR NAME, BUT I THINK WE WILL BE GOOD FRIENDS."** I smiled. I already liked Jade. The locket was beautiful. I felt bad for taking something so pretty and personal. I put the necklace on my dresser and made a mental note to give it back. I didn't want to take anything that she might have an emotional connection to.

The foods, however, were things like crackers, bars, and cookies. Majority of them were sweet. It had been a long time since I had something sweet. I stared at the food for a long moment before deciding that I would eat them later. I didn't want to give myself a cramp.

There was something in there that caught my attention. I reached the bottom of the box and pulled out several photos. There were pictures of Jason and Cameron. They looked like brothers. They were both smiling, and they stood very close to each other as they looked at the camera. The background was unfamiliar, so I guessed they took this before they had gotten here. Cameron and Jason knew each other before they got here?

Were they actually brothers? They didn't look alike. Maybe they were half siblings. They seemed to always be in sync with each other and Cameron cared a lot about Jason, and vice versa. I never thought about this until now and I didn't know how to feel about it. Jason and Cameron were definitely close... I just didn't know how close.

My mind was spinning. I looked toward the other box and had an enticing feeling to open it. I forced myself to put it under my bed. It was late, and I needed to sleep. I'd have to look at it tomorrow. I crawled into the bed and closed my eyes. I thought about all the things that happened today and saw that things were getting better for me. I was developing better relationships with everyone here and I was slowly learning more about everyone as they were of me. I was slowly opening up, which was what I was trying to do. I smiled to myself. I felt my body become heavier and I gracefully let sleep take me.

I looked at my mother as she quickly packed up our things. I watched as she and dad worked hastily. They seemed almost afraid. They left nothing behind in the places they rummaged through. I turned in circles as I watched them with a deep fascination. Why were they moving so fast? What was going on?

My mother looked at me and stopped packing. She kneeled down to my height and gently grabbed my shoulders and looked me straight in the eye. "Honey, we have to go now."

"Where are we going?" I asked softly.

"I can't say. We are going somewhere far away from here, but you can't come." My mother said sadly.

"Why not, mommy?"

"Just...where we are going, you cannot come. It's too dangerous to take you with us...you have to stay here. We will make sure you have a wonderful family that will take care of you. I promise we will come back someday."

I felt tears in my eyes. I didn't really understand, but I had a bad feeling that was gnawing at my stomach. I could feel that I would never see them again. My mother was saying goodbye. She had promised me they would come back, but I didn't know how long it would take for that day to come.

My mom kissed my cheek and stood up. She walked over to my dad and he quickly took their bags. My father stopped and gave me a quick hug and kiss, then stepped out the door. My mother went to follow him, but turned back to me. She looked at me sadly and mouthed, "I love you." She blew me a kiss, and I saw her eyes glisten with tears. As she walked out, my entire world exploded with light.

*   *   *   *

I woke up with a start. What the hell was that? I didn't really remember that, but I figured that it was buried somewhere in my subconscious, along with the other memories I didn't want to have. I looked out the window and saw light shine through the cracks of the blinds. I rubbed my eyes and looked at my clock to see it was 8:24 in the morning.

It was way earlier than I normally woke, but I knew I would not go back to sleep soon. I took the covers off of me and sat up. When my mind cleared, I remembered the box underneath my bed. I dropped to the floor and looked for the small blue box Alice had given me. I sat back on the bed and stared at the momentum I held. I was almost afraid to open it. What if I saw something I would wish I hadn't? After taking a deep breath, I slowly opened the box and looked at what was inside. There were pictures of me and my parents, cards I had made for holidays, gifts my parents had given me, and a few things from Alice and my other foster parents from past years.

Each time I went to a new home, I would collect one or two things and put them in this box so I would have something of my past to remember. It was another thing I had to show where I had come from. While looking at the trinkets, I took nothing out. I just lifted them, studied what I held, and gently put it back. I didn't want to lose anything. When I was finished picking through my past, I put the box back underneath my bed and went downstairs.

It was quiet, and I thought I was the only one awake. I took advantage of the quiet to tour the house a little more. First thing that I looked at were the walls. There were pictures of Hayley and the kids. One picture was of her and all of them; Hayley and Aliyah; Hayley with Jade and Aliyah; Hayley with Jason and Cameron; and Hayley with a man I didn't recognize.

They all were side-by-side on the wall in order by age. I walked to the unfurnished room with the things hanging from the ceiling. They looked like paper crafts a kid makes in school. One of them was a painting of a rainbow and another was a small hand with, *I WOVE WU MOMMY*, written on it. I guessed that the work was Aliyah's.

"How long have you been up?"

I gasped and spun around to see Hayley looking at me with curious eyes.

"Um, not very long. I just wanted to look around. Where is everyone?" I asked, breathlessly.

"They have school. I kept them out when I found out when you were coming, but I had to send them back before we all got in trouble." Hayley giggled.

"Oh, well, what will we do today, then?" I asked, frowning.

"Well, here's the thing: I actually enrolled you in school with them." Hayley admitted.

"Today? Now? Where? Why?" I asked. School? What's the point in me going there?

"All kids under 18 need to go to school or I would be incarcerated, Kassey. I think you know that. You are going to Chesterway high. It's the same place Jason and Cameron go. I enrolled you in 10th grade classes." Hayley explained. I could tell that she wanted to say, "It's the same place your brothers go," but she held herself back. "I already got you everything you would need. You just need to get yourself ready and I'll take you there." Hayley continued.

I stared at her for a moment before nodding and heading to my room to get changed. I stood in my room, pacing back and forth. Why would I have to go to school? The last time I did, I got expelled for getting involved in a fight, and it wasn't even my fault! I settled on faded, blue ripped jeans and a plain black t-shirt. When I was finished, I ran down the stairs to where Hayley waited with my schoolbag. When she made sure everything was situated, she hauled me out the door and to the car. Hayley got into the driver's side and me in the passenger's side. My foster mother started the car, and we both headed for the school.

*   *   *   *

It was a huge school, as it seemed to wrap around a whole block. The parking lot was just as big and was filled with cars of different sizes and brands. Hayley drove up to the front of the school and left the car idling.

"So, are you ready? Do you have everything you need?" Hayley asked.

"Yes, I have my bag, papers, and other things you gave me." I said, while reaching behind me for my school bag.

Hayley smiled, then pulled me into a hug. It didn't last very long. When she pulled away, I got out of the car and headed toward the front doors. When I looked back, I saw her car driving out of the parking lot.

It took me a little while to find the front office, but when I did, they couldn't find my schedule. I have never been more irritated in my life. It took them 15 minutes to find my schedule, check me in, and go over the map to find where I was supposed to go.

When I got out of the office, the hallway was filled with students trying to get to their next class. I had to push my way through the tsunami until I reached my math class.

I was one of the first kids to come into the classroom. The teacher was sitting at his desk reading a book. I walked up to him, but he didn't seem to notice me. I knocked on the desk and he lifted his head to look at me with a bored expression.

"Yes?" His voice was scratchy.

"I'm new here. I was told to let you know." I said. The woman in the office told me to let every teacher know I was new so I could be in the system.

He looked at me for a moment before checking his computer. "Oh, yeah. Here you are... Kassey?"

"Yes. I'm... Kassey." I said awkwardly. I looked at his desk and saw that his nametag read Mr. Felix.

The teacher, Mr. Felix, checked me in and sat me in an empty seat close to the back of the classroom. I unpacked my papers and books that Hayley gave me and spread them on the desk. I heard the chair move next to me and I lifted my head to see a girl that looked to be the same age as me, maybe a little older. She had hazel eyes and her hair was pitch black with red highlights. She had a soft face that was purely feminine and young. She smiled at me when I caught her eye.

"I don't think I've seen you here before. Are you new?" Her voice was kinda low but still had a high pitch.

"Um, yeah, I just got here today. I'm Kassey." I said.

"Brianna. Nice to meet you. I hope we can be friends." Brianna smiled and turned towards the front of the room when the teacher started instruction.

"So, how are you liking your first day?" Brianna asked as we walked to her locker.

"Well, I almost got trampled in the hallway and it took forever for them to find my schedule and give me ideas of where to go." I said, remembering the struggle I went through about an hour ago.

Brianna laughed. "I've been there, but you survived! Also, you get to go to lunch now since you kinda missed your first class. After lunch, do you want me to tour you?" Brianna asked me as she switched out her things.

"Yeah, I think I need that. Thanks." I said, relieved.

"No problem. What are friends for?" Brianna said, shrugging. I smiled. I made my first friend.

"Kassey?"

I turned around to a familiar voice and found Cameron staring at me with a look of confusion. I blinked, and it took me a moment to remember who he was.

"Cameron! Hey. I can explain."

"Hayley enrolled you in our school, didn't she?" Cameron said matter-of-factly.

"Y-yeah. Um, Cameron, this is Brianna. Brianna, this is Cameron." I introduced them.

"Hello." Brianna dragged the word out. When I looked back at her, I saw her looking at Cameron with a weird expression. "Kassey, I'll meet you in the lunchroom, alright?" She slammed her locker shut and left without giving me a chance to respond. What was that about?

"Don't worry about her. She doesn't really like me. We used to date, and I broke up with her because she was too much drama." Cameron said, snickering.

"You dated? Wow...well, she doesn't seem to be someone for drama." I said, looking at the direction Brianna had gone.

"Well, trust me, she is. I won't tell you not to hang out with her. Just one piece of advice: Don't bring your dates around her. She acts differently." Cameron said with a frown.

"Thanks for the advice."

"No, problem. Let's go. I usually sit with Jason and the guys. I want to see his face when he sees you come in." Cameron nudged me towards the cafeteria.

It was really loud, and there were long lines of people buying food. I didn't even want to waste the energy to partake in that. Cameron saw my face. "I'll buy you lunch."

"Cam—"

"Look, you can't keep skipping. Plus, I doubt mother gave you any money, so I'll buy you something. If you don't like it, give it to the guys. They'll gladly take it." Cameron pressed.

I didn't know what else to say. I was still on the part where Cam had called Hayley "mother." I don't think he even noticed. I stopped arguing with him and let him buy my food. Cameron showed me where the table was and I made my way past the crowded tables to where Jason and his friends were. They all looked up at me and Jason's face showed multiple emotions. The only one I caught was shock.

"Kassey? What are you doing here?" Jason moved his things so I could sit down.

I put my things down next to me as I sat down. "Hayley enrolled me in school. I woke up and saw that no one else was there."

"Sorry about that. It was a normal schedule. I would've told you but I didn't think you were up yet." Jason said apologetically then asked, "Where's Cam?"

"It's fine, and um, Cameron's buying me lunch." I must have sounded horrified because Jason's face turned into a frown that was kind of identical to the ones Cameron gives me.

"You worried he'll poison you?" Jason said jokingly.

"No, not really."

"Hey Jace, are you going to introduce us or pretend we aren't here?" One guy cut in, sounding irritated.

"Oh, right. Kassey, these are my guys: Jessie, Daniel, and Jett. Guys, this is Kassey. Hayley adopted her a few days ago." Jason explained.

I looked at him sharply and I saw him recoil. Why did he openly say that? I never told people I was a foster child and Hayley *didn't* adopt me! *Not yet*, I thought. Well, I wasn't letting myself get my hopes up. I just didn't like the reactions I got when people found out I was a foster. It was the type of reactions that made you wish you had said nothing.

"Kass—"

I jumped up from the table and started walking towards the doors of the cafe. I felt my skin get hot as my temper flared. I felt like telling people you were a foster child was like putting a label on yourself. Jason telling them so easily and fast was like a slap in the face for me. I preferred to keep my personal life to myself and think of excuses later.

"Kassey!" Jason grabbed my arm and spun me around to face him. His face showed sadness and regret. I sat there fuming at him with my arms crossed, trying to calm myself down.

"What?"

"What happened? Why did you run off like that?"

I huffed for a second before answering. "I don't enjoy telling people I'm fostered. I never have. It gives unwanted attention." My voice turned to a near whisper as I explained.

Jason stared at me for a moment. "Has something happened?"

"I lose many people when they find out I don't have what they have, a stable family. All I have are court papers and a box filled with valuables." I felt prickles behind my eyes and I bit my tongue to hold the tears back.

"You have us, Kassey. You're not by yourself. Hayley will adopt you."

"No, she won't! No one ever has. I just move somewhere in the world with new hopes of staying and then having them crushed all over again! I don't belong anywhere!" I yelled. By now, people were looking at us.

"Shh...that's not true. Not everyone is like that. You don't move forever. I can't say I know what it's like, but Hayley isn't the type of person to turn someone away. I promise you that." Jason said confidently. He searched my eyes, hoping I believed him.

I didn't know how to feel at that moment. Many memories and thoughts came to the front of my mind that I didn't want to remember. The things I had buried over the years threatened to tear free. My tears escaped despite me trying to hold them back. Jason's confusion turned to alarm, and he moved towards me, but I stepped back.

"Hey, what's going on?" Cameron walked over with two trays of food in his hands.

I looked at the two of them and wiped my face before turning on my heel and leaving the cafe. I heard the brother's call my name, but I ignored them. I needed to be alone.

CHAPTER SIX

Everything seemed to spin out of control. I was pacing on the side of the parking lot, trying to get myself under control. My tears wouldn't hold back and they kept streaming down my face when I would wipe them away. I knew I should've stayed in the cafeteria with the others, but I couldn't. My life wasn't like theirs. I felt like I was a totally different person in their lives trying to be like them, and it wasn't working.

I saw someone get out of a car and start heading in my direction. I could tell it was a boy, but I couldn't really see that good from where I was. It surprised me he kept coming towards me. Was I in the way of where he was going or did he want to see me? He then stopped a few feet away. The boy had on sunglasses and a black hoodie, so I couldn't really see his face. His hands were in his pockets and he stood really still. He was very tall and seemed to be older than I was.

"Hello." He said in a deep voice. It sounded familiar, but I didn't know why.

"Hey." I said politely. I couldn't see his eyes, but I knew they were staring holes in mine.

"I've never seen you here before. Did you just get here?" He asked curiously.

"Yeah, it's my first day. Um, do you normally get here this late?" I asked, just realizing that half the day had gone.

He shrugged. "Always. I don't really care about this place. I just come and go when the feeling presents itself." He took off his sunglasses and my heart sank. I knew him.

"Y-you…"

"I can't believe you forgot me, Kassey. I feel hurt." His name is Khalil. He was a foster brother I had a few years ago. I had never been more happy to leave that home and never look back. Khalil took a few steps towards me and I jumped back.

"Khalil...don't." I tripped on the curb on the sidewalk in my hurry to get away from him.

"Don't be afraid of me, Kassey. I haven't seen you in a while. We all miss you. I didn't want you to leave." Khalil kept coming closer until I slapped him. It was hard enough to make him stumble and stop to touch his cheek. I stood there shaking and waiting to see what he would do. He lifted his head and looked at me with anger in his eyes. I screamed and started running and I knew he was following. I didn't know exactly where I was running to. I just knew that I had to get away from this boy. Khalil was the person who destroyed my life years ago. I worked so hard to forget him, and just when I do that, he shows up at my school! What are the odds?

"Stop running, Kassey!"

I kept running and running until someone yanked me back and felt something crush my ribcage. I gasped and clenched my teeth together against the pain. I had slowed down and Khalil wrapped his arms around me to keep me from going anywhere. He whipped me around and his arms tightened at my sides. He slammed me on the ground and the air left my lungs. Khalil stood there, watching me as I struggled to stand up. When I would get far enough off the ground, he would clock me in the head with his elbow and knock me down again. After a few tries, and a few bruises, I gave up.

"What do you want?" It hurt to talk. I knew he would not kill me. Not here where people could see.

"I told you. I missed you. We all did. You were never supposed to leave. Amelia was going to be your home. You know that." Khalil said.

"I didn't want to remember you, Khalil. I never want to go back. I want you to leave me alone. I'm happy. I was happy when I left you. I don't want to go back." I was on the verge of tears by now, but I didn't want to show him any vulnerability. I slowly backed away from him until my back hit a tree. Khalil grabbed my wrist forcefully and yanked me up. My head spun from the fast movement, and a wave of nausea and dizziness hit me. I tried pulling my hand from his grip, but he was strong.

"I never forgot about you. You never did either. You knew who I was as soon as I came to you. I never left your memory." Khalil whispered in my ear, and I shivered. He was close enough that I felt his body heat. He moved my hair to the side and kissed my neck. I stood there frozen in fear. I wanted to push him away, but I didn't want to spark his temper. We stood like that until I worked up the courage to kneel him in his stomach.

Khalil grunted and loosened his grip on my wrist. Taking advantage of his pain, I took off running again. It hurt like hell, but I needed to put some distance between me and him.

I ran into the school and found, to my dismay, that the hallways were empty. I panicked. Where was he? Was there someone I could run to? I looked out the door to see him still coming towards me. My brain didn't seem to want to work, and I did not know what to do. My body hurt, and I was breathing way too fast. Everything was spinning.

"Kassey?"

I turned and saw Cameron coming into the hallway. I had never been more happy to hear his voice! I was about to run to him when I felt a grip on my wrist and my fear flooded back in. I screamed, forgetting that I was indoors, and whipped around wildly. Cameron rushed towards me and pulled us both apart.

"What the hell is going on?" Cameron's eyes were wild.

I shook my head vigorously. "Please get him away from me!" I hid behind Cameron.

Khalil took one look at Cam and backed up. Whatever his face showed, it seemed to make Khalil think twice about what he was going to do. The boy glared at me one last time before slowly leaving the school. Cameron and I stood there for a moment before he turned to me.

"Kassey, please tell me what happened. You're bleeding and bruised. Who was that?" Cameron rambled.

"I-I..." I still couldn't make my brain work to form the right words. I couldn't take my eyes away from the door. I felt like, if I turned around, he may come back and everything would continue again. Maybe even worse.

Cameron looked at me with nervousness. "Kassey, please talk to me."

I took a deep breath before trying to speak. "His n-name is K-Khalil. He used to be my f-foster brother a few y-years ago. I didn't like that home and I-I didn't like him."

"He seems violent. What happened? Did he attack you?"

"Y-yeah, I didn't even know who he was at first until he took off his glasses, but he knew exactly who I was." I felt hot and cold all over. I couldn't slow my breathing, and I didn't feel like I was standing upright. Cameron looked at me with a worried expression.

"I think you need to go get checked out."

"Like a hospital? N-no, no way. I'm not going." I protested.

"Kassey, something could be seriously wrong. Just do it. I'll take you there."

"What about Jason?"

"I'll text him on the way."

I hesitated for a moment, but my body screamed for me to lie down. I nodded to Cam, and he took me to his car and drove me to the hospital.

CHAPTER SEVEN

We were there for a while. The doctors checked me and said I had a mild concussion and bruising. They told me to lie down for a while and let my body rest.

Cameron never left the room when the doctor was present and he still hadn't left when the doctor exited. He texted Jason and told me that Jason was coming. I was really worried about Hayley's reaction. What would she think? I haven't been here for a week and I have already landed in the hospital! I fell asleep a few times since the doctors laid me down. Cameron brought me food and drink from the cafe and I gladly ate it. It was absolutely horrible, but my body was glad to have something to eat.

Jason burst in the door and looked between us. His eyes stopped at mine and I sat there frozen. That was a face I didn't want to see. I didn't want to make anyone worry.

"Are you alright? What happened?" Jason asked as he came into the room.

"She has a mild concussion and bruises. They stitched her up, so she's no longer bleeding." Cameron explained.

Jason's eyes flared. "Someone attacked you?" I could tell he was working hard to keep himself under control.

"Jason—"

"The truth, Kassey."

I sighed. "Yes, but you don't know him. His name is Khalil. He was a foster brother I had a few years ago. It wasn't the best family I've had, and I never wanted to go back." I explained.

"So, how did he find you? Have you talked to him or the family since you left?" Cameron asked.

"No, he said he went to school there." I pulled out my phone and showed them a picture of him. I meant to delete it, but I could never bring myself to. Something always held me back, no matter how badly I wanted to be rid of him.

The brothers stared at the picture. "He looks familiar. He goes to the school. I have a class with him. He skips a lot." Jason said.

"Yeah, I do, too. He wasn't here today. Did he know where you went to school?" Cameron asked as he gave me my phone back.

"No, I just came today, so no one would really know...but then, Khalil was very smart and had ways of finding things out, so he may have known. It hurts to think that much." I said, rubbing my head against the throbbing headache that was building.

"Don't stress yourself out, Kassey. We'll figure it out." Jason said.

There was a knock on the door, and we all turned to see Hayley and the doctor came into the room. My heart dropped when I saw her face. Hayley was the last person I wanted to see while I was here. She talked to the boys while the doctor examined me.

Aliyah and Jade walked in behind her. I saw that their faces had tears streaked on them when they looked at me. I felt my heart tighten when I looked at them. It hurt to see them like that because of me.

"I would like to speak to Kassey for a moment." Hayley said. She sounded different from the way she had the first few days I have known her. It made me more nervous. When Cameron, Jason, the girls, and the doctor cleared the room, Hayley sat at the foot of the bed. She looked at me for a while before she said anything.

"What happened?"

"My former foster brother attacked me." I said. I tried to sum it up in a semi-ok and not-so-concerning way.

"Who was it? How did he know where you were?" Hayley pressed.

"His name is Khalil, and I don't know how he knew where I was. Didn't Cameron or Jason tell you what happened?" I asked. Did they call her here saying nothing to me about it?

"No, they didn't call me. Ms. Reynolds told me you were here when the hospital contacted her. When they checked you in, it showed that you were a foster child since your file was already in the government system. It was legal business to call me themselves." Hayley explained.

"Oh..listen Hayley—"

"Don't. Don't, Kassey." She cut me off.

"Please don't be mad, ok? I didn't mean for any of this to happen. I don't know how he found me, and I never wanted to see him again." I said pleadingly.

"Why would he even try to hurt you? Why was he violent? What happened between you two?" Hayley asked, boring holes in my eyes.

My breathing quickened. "Please don't make me say it."

"Kassey, tell me, now. Why did he try to hurt you? Did he have a reason?"

The whole family was in the room by now. I hadn't even noticed they had come back in. The boys were looking at me as intensively as Hayley was, while the girls were looking confused.

"You can tell us, Kassey. You trust us, right?" Jason asked.

I slowly nodded. The words slowly made their way out of my mouth, but it didn't really feel like I had said it. However, everyone's faces showed the opposite.

"Khalil raped me."

CHAPTER EIGHT

Everyone stared at me with horrified expressions. No one said anything for a while. They all just stared at me.

"What does "'raped'" mean?" Aliyah asked suddenly.

"Nevermind that, Aliyah." Hayley said firmly.

"Kassey, why didn't you say anything about this before?" Cameron asked.

"Y-you don't just go walking around telling people you let someone take advantage of you and you didn't do a damn thing about it! It's not a simple thing to talk about." I grunted as the headache came back in a bigger form.

Jason went out to find the doctor and Cameron grabbed a cup off of the counter and gave me some water. After I finished the water, the doctor came in and examined me.

"Her blood pressure is too high. She needs rest. I'm going to ask all of you to leave." She said.

Everyone looked at each other before filing out of the room. I closed my eyes, but sleep never came. Every time I closed my eyes, I could see the attack repeatedly. It felt more real each time I saw it and soon; I wasn't even able to relax. Throughout the next couple of hours, the doctor examined me a few more times before saying it was ok for me to go home. Hayley signed me out and we all rode back to the house.

*   *   *   *

It was dinnertime, and Hayley told us she was in the middle of preparing when she got the call. She sat us all down in the living room and told us to wait. I could tell her mood was low, and I didn't want to do anything to make things worse than they seemed to be, so I kept my mouth shut and did what she asked. Everyone was nice to me all afternoon by making sure I was comfortable, not piling questions on me, and making sure they didn't hover too much.

While waiting for dinner, I was about to head to my room when I heard someone call my name. Hayley was at the sink washing the dishes, but she motioned for me to come over. I slowly made my way towards her with my guard up. What was on her mind?

"Hayley—"

"I'm not mad." She cut me off.

"You're not?" I raised an eyebrow.

Hayley smiled. "No, I got scared. I didn't know what happened and...to get a call from the hospital…" She trailed off, looking at me with a troubled expression.

"Well, it's nice to be cared about. Um, do you need help?" I asked. I wanted to get off the topic while everything was good.

"No, everything has already been taken care of. Do you want to go to school tomorrow? I understand if you don't. I'll tell them some excuse." Hayley suggested.

"No, I'm not shrinking away just because something bad happened. I'm fine." I said that but felt like he burned me with hellfire. I guess I was hiding my discomfort well since she said nothing...or maybe she saw but didn't want to press the issue. My foster mother had us set the table, and we all ate in comfortable silence.

After dinner, I went for a walk. I needed to feel the chilly breeze on my hot skin. I needed to think things through. I stopped by an oak tree and closed my eyes as I leaned against its bark. The sky was darkening, and the sun was setting. When I was little, I would climb onto my window and watch the sunset and disappear, until the sky turned dark. It was my favorite thing to do at night, besides reading the notes and looking at the things my parents left me. They both mattered a lot.

"Hey."

I opened my eyes to see Jason staring at me. He wasn't right in front of me, but he was leaning against the side of the tree. I didn't know how long he had been there, but he looked pretty comfortable as he watched me.

"Did you follow me here?" I asked.

"Kinda, Hayley had said you left the house saying nothing and—"

"She was worried." I finished for him and followed with a sigh.

"For good reason. After what happened today, everyone may be a little on edge for a while. It's what they do." Jason explained.

"How do you feel?" I asked.

"I want to find the bastard, but the last thing I need to do is make things harder for you." Jason walked up to me. I couldn't really see his face, but I saw an outline of a smile.

I smiled back. "Jason, did you feel the same way Cameron felt when I first came here?" I was afraid of his answer, so I waited for him to think.

"I didn't hate you, if that's what you mean. I wanted to get to know you and I be the most inviting one, other than Aliyah." He said with a chuckle.

"Aliyah is a little angel. She's been nice, but she's kinda mature for a seven-year-old." I said, remembering the way she talked at the amusement park.

"She's been in foster care since she was born. I don't think she even knows her parents. She's been to one other home than ours and it wasn't really her favorite because she only stayed there till she turned three." Jason said. His face showed a bit of anger before it passed. I wanted to ask, but decided against it. It was in the past and I didn't want to dredge up terrible memories. When Jason decided it was late enough for us to go back inside, he took my hand and led me back to the house.

CHAPTER NINE

The next morning was my second day of school. Hayley asked me again if I wanted to stay home, and I assured her I was fine enough to go. My head still hurt, and it was a struggle to get out of bed, but I was determined not to let that stop me. I've experienced pain worse than this, plus, I was a fighter. We all rode in Cameron's car since he was the only one, other than Hayley, who had a car. He told me that Hayley's husband gave it to him before he drafted himself and left. Plus, Cameron was two months older than Jason, so they gave him the privilege of a car first. Cameron dropped Aliyah and Jade off at their elementary school, and he took us to our high school.

Cam parked the car, and Jason tried to help me out. I took his hand and smiled at him. When we walked into the building, I had to stop myself from looking around. The building was still huge and swarming with students trying to find their classes.

"Do you know where you're going?" Jason asked me when we got into the building.

"Um, a little. I didn't really finish yesterday." I said, remembering me storming out and landing in the hospital for the rest of the day. I had only been to one class, not including lunch.

"Do you need any help?"

"I'm sure I can figure it out. You two go. I don't want to make you late." I said, looking for my schedule.

"Kassey..." Cameron said hesitantly.

"I'm fine. Go." I said firmly. I didn't enjoy hovering and I couldn't stand it when they wouldn't leave me alone. I know now how to make sure nothing happens to me. I know how to protect myself. Cameron and Jason went off to their classes, and I walked around to find mine.

After a few minutes of struggling, I found my psychology class, but was late, as told by the teacher. He sent me to an empty seat with a warning and introduced himself as Mr. Holden. For an hour and a half, we learned about the reasons people do what they do and how certain things affect us mentally. We learned the extremes of trauma and were quizzed on the personalities and actions that can result from psychological errors. I stared at the teacher in disbelief. It was my first day in this class and I was being *quizzed* on *this*? I then remembered that school had already started, and I was late for enrollment.

I was staring at my paper when I felt a tap on my arm. I looked up at the boy sitting next to me. He wasn't looking at me, but turned my way when he saw me staring.

He was caramel skinned with bright brown eyes. His chestnut hair was cropped short and had auburn highlights. He wore a plain grey shirt and black pants with rips in the knees.

"Sorry. I—uh, I didn't mean to touch you." He apologized. His voice was the voice of a sixteen or seventeen-year-old. It had adolescence but was still kinda high. He had a little slur and the sound of an accent in his words like he hadn't been speaking English for very long.

"Oh, um, it's fine. I do not know what I'm doing, anyway." I admitted with a little smile.

He smiled back. "I'm Eván."

"I'm Kassey." I must have sounded hesitant, because he tilted his head.

"You seem like the quiet type."

"I'm more of a 'suffer in silence' type." I shrugged.

Evan laughed but looked confused. "Are you new here?"

"Since yesterday. I'm still trying to find my way, but I think I'm doing good for a newcomer." I joked.

"Well, I'd be happy to show you the ropes. If you like. I'll tell you all the things you need to know at Chesterway alto." Evan's smile grew bigger.

I squinted at him. Did he say Chesterway alto? "Thanks? I think I would like that." I drawled out.

"Cool," He looked over at my paper, "That one is wrong. The heart doesn't need the brain to function."

"Thanks." I scoffed and fixed my answer. I guess I had just made another friend.

After the bell rang, everyone hurried out of the classroom. I packed my things and watched as Evan did the same. I called out to him as he started to walk out.

"Yeah?"

"Um, thanks for the help. It was nice to know someone else here." I said lamely.

"No problemo. If you need anything else then just let me know." He started to leave again then turned back around. "Will you be at lunch?"

"I don't eat lunch, but I will be there, yeah."

"I usually drive out and buy lunch. If you want to join, then meet me outside by lunchtime." Evan said before walking out of the classroom.

*   *   *   *

I made it to my next class in a daze. What the hell just happened? My first conversation ended in being invited to lunch. I didn't know if I was more happy or nervous. Brianna noticed the change in my attitude and immediately pounced.

"What's up?"

"Um…" I tried to figure out if I should tell her or not. I remembered what Cameron told me about her being a lot of drama, especially with boys.

"Tell me, Kassey. Something is on your mind. Spill it!"

I sighed. "Do you know anyone named Evan?"

"Evan Revera? Yeah, he's cute. Why?"

"Well, he's in my psychology class and he kinda invited me to ride and get lunch." I confessed.

"What?! That's amazing! What did you say?" Brianna's voice level got louder.

"I didn't answer. It was a kind of, 'meet me at this place as an answer,' thing. He left before I *could* answer. Plus, Brianna, I don't eat lunch. It would be a waste."

"Nonsense! Pretend you want something from where you are going. Don't you dare flake out! This is how relationships get started, Kassey! Don't mess it up by not going. What reason do you have to reject it?" Brianna asked firmly.

I tried to think of an excuse, then sighed in defeat. "None."

"Exactly. You have no reason to say no, so you are going. That is that. Finished. *Finito.* Done." Brianna winked at me and turned towards the front of the room when the teacher started instruction.

After a boring hour of the many ways to use pie, we got dismissed for lunch. My heart was beating like a drum the whole time I packed up. Brianna talked to me the entire way to her locker. I think it was her way of trying to calm me down when she saw how wound up I was.

"So, you're not going?"

"I want to...I just don't know if I should." Boys weren't exactly my strong suit. I may have a wall up with everyone, but my wall was higher with boys. Personal and past reasons.

"Look, do whatever you want, but I think you will regret it if you don't go." I stared at her. "Do you trust me?" She asked when I didn't answer.

"Yeah, I trust you." I said truthfully.

"Then trust me on this. If it turns out to be a disaster, then I will owe you for a week. Scout's honor." She placed her hand over her heart and smiled at me.

I smiled back at her. "Will you tell Cameron so he doesn't flip?"

Brianna giggled. "Yes, don't worry about him. He's overprotective of you. I don't why." She shrugged.

"Yeah, well." I didn't fully answer, and I hoped she didn't notice. "See you later, Brianna." I said and quickly headed towards the entrance of the school.

*   *   *   *

It was warmer outside than I was used to. I had worn a black leather jacket over a tank top and short-shorts. I normally don't wear shorts because of the visible marks on my skin. Through the years, some of the foster parents and siblings I had were abusive, but I had pleasant homes, too. I was just sick of being in a *temporary* home. I liked my leather jacket because it was something Alice had given me because she knew I liked black and leather clothing. I always wore it with an outfit whenever I could.

I closed my eyes and felt the sun on my face. I always enjoyed the heat better than the cold. The parking lot was filled top to bottom with cars and trucks. The sun shone down on them, making them shine like diamonds. I breathed in the humid air and smiled a little to myself. I let myself forget for a moment why I had come out. Then, I felt a tap on my shoulder and I opened my eyes to see who had caught me here.

Evan smiled when he saw me focus on him. He had his hands in his pockets and had changed to a black tank top that showed more of his muscular shape. I didn't realize I was staring until he cleared his throat and I moved my eyes away from his figure.

"I wasn't sure you would show." He said.

"I wasn't sure, either."

"Why did you?"

"You seemed like a nice guy...and I wanted to have some fun. I wanted to hang out with a friend. I don't have many." I said sadly.

"Well, let me be the amigó that brings you fun." Evan clapped his hands together and laughed maniacally.

I raised an eyebrow. "Are you a comic book geek?"

"No, ew, never." He rolled his eyes. "Shall we get going?"

"Yeah. Lead the way." I nodded.

Evan walked ahead of me toward his car and I followed. He had a black sedan that looked very polished and very taken care of. He got in the driver's side and I got into the passenger's. When Evan slowly left the parking lot and got onto the road, I asked where we were going.

"Well, we have half an hour, so we can do whatever we want. First, we get food." Evan responded while still looking forward.

Evan gave me a list of places to choose from in the area. I just told him to go wherever he wanted.

"I don't want anything."

He sighed, annoyed. "Do you always do this?" He turned to me with a disappointed look.

"Do what?"

"Skip."

"Yeah. Whenever I feel like it. It's become normal." I answered nonchalantly.

"That's not good." He said, repeating what Jason remarked the first time I told them.

"Well, that's just how I live my life."

"Are you vegana?" Evan pressed.

"What?" I turned to look at him, confused.

"Vegana, um...you eat different foods than others." He tried to explain.

"I don't eat meat, no. I've had alternatives. Meat just makes you sick." I rambled.

"Meat doesn't make everyone sick. Maybe just you. It's alright. We'll find something." Evan said confidently.

We drove the rest of the way in silence. Evan told me about a Mongolian restaurant, but he wouldn't tell me what it was called. I saw the parking lot was filled when we pulled in. I sat up and tried to read the restaurant's sign through the windshield, but I couldn't understand the language or the symbols. Evan shut off the car's engine and got out of the car. I waited a moment before following him out.

When we got in, the server sat us at a table. We sat across from each other and looked through the menus in silence. I got more and more confused as I flipped through the pages. What was this stuff? Most of the food didn't even look edible.

I heard a laugh and looked up to see Evan's face brighten with laughter.

I crossed my arms and looked at him through slit eyes. "What?"

"Your face was priceless." He chortled.

"Well, I do not know what any of this is." I complained.

"Well, since you have a limited amount of what you can eat, I think I know what to order you." Evan said as he went back to his menu.

The server came to the table and pulled out a notepad. "Are you two ready to order?"

"Yes, she'll have the Boortsog with rice and red beans." Evan responded while looking at the list of food.

I gave him a weird look, but he didn't see it. Was he trying to poison me?

"And you?" The server asked Evan.

"I'll do the Mutton Buuz and a beer. Would you be able to give a few little bottles of vodka on the side?" Evan asked with a smirk.

The server smiled and nodded. "Do you want anything to drink?" He asked me.

"I'll just have water."

After the server left, I said, "Beer and vodka?"

"I need a release. Plus, they are *way* stronger than vino. I don't do that." Evan shrugged.

I do not know what this boy says sometimes. "You are too much. You ordered like you knew exactly what was on the menu."

"Well, I come here during lunch sometimes. The people here know me. It's become my favorite place."

My phone buzzed in my pocket, and I fished it out. Cameron had texted me to let me know Brianna had told him where I was. The text also said, *"Don't worry about anyone or anything else. You just worry about having fun. If he hurts you, I will kill him myself."* I rolled my eyes but smiled to myself. This was a big step from where we were. Before, Cameron couldn't have cared less about how I felt. Now, he was always looking for ways to protect me.

"Kassey." I heard loud snapping.

I blinked and looked up at Evan's serious face. "What? What's wrong?"

"Was it something important? I'll let you call them." Evan suggested.

"No, it's fine." I quickly texted Cam a reply and put my phone away. "I didn't come here to text."

Evan's face turned back into a smile. Our food came later and Evan watched me as I took a bite of the Boortsog. I looked up at him when I was halfway through spoonfuls.

"So...?"

"Maybe it's good." I said stubbornly.

Evan chuckled. "You can be like that, but I know you love it."

"It's definitely a different type of food." I looked at his many bottles of alcohol and watched as he poured some of them into his beer. "Are you trying to get drunk before we get back in...ten minutes?"

He choked on his beer. "Ten minutes?"

"Yep. Ten minutes, so I think it would be a good idea to put down the bottle and stay sober. You still have two and a half hours of school left." I told him.

Evan groaned. "That was unnecessary, Kassey."

"It was very necessary." I saw the server and signaled for the check.

The server gave us the check, and Evan stopped me when I pulled money out of my bag.

"What are you doing?"

"We need money, right?" I asked, confused. I had money already in my hand, ready to be put down.

"Yeah, not from you. The reason I asked you to come with me wasn't so you could pay." Evan shook his head.

I was always used to paying for myself when I went out. My foster parents would pay sometimes, but I learned how to take care of myself from a young age. I got used to not relying on others. "Evan—"

"Nope. Nope. Nope. Put it away." Evan said dismissively.

I stared at him until he crossed his arms and his light brown eyes seemed to darken and pierce into mine. I figured he was really serious, so I put the money away and let him take care of lunch.

Evan drove us back to the school just when the warning bell rang. We hadn't finished all of our food, but Evan figured we didn't really need to bring anything with us, so we left it at the restaurant. We rushed into the building and saw the last groups of kids running to their classes.

"So, are you glad you went?" Evan asked me as we stood outside of my classroom.

"Yeah, I'm really glad I went." I could feel myself smiling and I willed myself to stop before I embarrassed myself.

Evan smiled. "I had fun with you today, Kassey. Let me know when you want to hang out again."

"Yeah, I will."

"See you later." Evan winked at me and walked down the hall. I watched him until he disappeared around a corner. I tried to catch my breath before walking into the classroom.

*   *   *   *

I waited outside for Cameron and Jason at the end of the school day and since I rode to school with them. I couldn't stop thinking about my lunch with Evan. How could one conversation go so far? I never thought I would enjoy it the way I did, but I had to remind myself why I separate myself from people—boys—in the first place. I didn't want to end up hurt and having to start over.

Cameron picked up the girls and drove all of us home. I didn't have homework, so I just went to my room and threw down my bag. My head was still going through what happened at lunch. Was that just him being friendly, or was it something else? Did I want it to be something else? I shook my head and got up from the bed, then suddenly had a weird feeling of wanting to look under my bed. When I did, I saw nothing wrong until I realized that someone had moved the blue box. Where was it? It was the only thing under my bed and I always put it either in the middle or by the wall. Now, it wasn't in either spot and I knew I put it there yesterday or this morning. I jumped up and ran to my drawer where I kept my parent's note. I realized that was missing, too. Where the hell were my things?! I got angry, but I was also afraid. I needed those things, like I needed air to breathe.

I ran down the stairs and into each room, where I completely made them a wreck. I couldn't find them wherever I looked. Tears streamed down my face. This was a complete nightmare. Where were they? Who was in my room?

"Hey! Kassey, stop!" Arms grabbed my waist and pulled me back. I whipped wildly against them until they released me. Jason stared at me with a bewildered expression. "What's going on? What are you doing?"

"Leave me alone!" I pushed past him and ran to the playroom. There were many things in there and I quickly looked through them.

"Kassey, stop! Calm down! Talk to me." Jason spun me around to face him.

I growled. "What the hell do you want?"

"What are you doing? You're making a colossal mess of the house—"

"I need to find something!" I turned back around to keep looking.

"What are you looking for? Maybe I can help."

"I don't want your help! I just want you to make yourself useful elsewhere where you're wanted and leave me the hell alone!" I screamed at him.

Jason's face dropped, and he turned away from me. Hayley and Jade came into the playroom behind him.

"What is all the yelling about?" Hayley asked sternly.

"Nothing." I said as nonchalantly as I could, but I knew I failed to sound calm.

"Kassey, you're making a mess..." Jade said accusingly.

I stopped and muttered, "It's not here."

"What's not here? What are you looking for?" Hayley asked.

I didn't answer them. I didn't tell anyone about the notes or my box. Even Jason didn't really know what was in it when he brought it to me. I wanted to keep that to myself, but if they were both missing, someone knew about them.

I pushed past everyone and ran outside. I ran and didn't stop. I didn't stop when my feet hurt. I didn't stop when my chest burned. I didn't stop when the tears returned. I didn't stop even when I was a few blocks away from the house. I wanted to be by myself and try to think. My things were missing. Everything had disappeared. I had told no one about them, hadn't I? I hid them, but since they were missing, someone knew where they were and everything about them. I just didn't know who knew and where they had put them. Maybe someone took them out of the house.

I finally stopped and fell to the ground. My strength left me and I crumbled in a defeated heap. My life was in those possessions I had. I kept them safe and guarded. I needed them to live on in the life I now had. Without them, I had nothing else at all. The sun shone bright above me, but I didn't feel the warmth. I felt the hole in my chest now more than ever. Now, as I sat on the ground in a place that I didn't know.

I had never felt more alone.

CHAPTER TEN

I woke up in my bed. I didn't know how or when I got back here. The last thing I remembered was being outside in a whole other neighborhood. It was dark outside, and the clock showed it was after midnight. How long had I been here? They swaddled me in my blankets and it took me a minute to get myself free. When I did, I saw I still had on my clothes from the day. I got up, slowly opened my door, and walked out.

The hallway was quiet, and every door was closed but one. I saw that Hayley's door was open at the end of the hall. I slowly made my way toward there and looked inside. It was quiet, but I could tell she was awake. When I stood there for a moment, she saw me and motioned for me to come in. I took my time approaching the bed. She was sitting up like someone who fell asleep while standing. I stood there for a moment and waited for her to speak.

"Cameron found you outside. You were a long way from here." She finally said.

I didn't respond. I wanted to know why she even cared whether I made it back. Why did any of them care? They could've left me out there and I would've been happy.

"Kassey, talk to me. What happened today? Why did you lash out like that? Jason was so upset when you left."

"I told him I didn't need help." I mumbled.

"You didn't need to treat him so badly. He cares about you. Everyone cares about you, even Cameron. Now, please tell me what you were looking for." Hayley restated.

"Something that was important to me. It isn't where I left it."

"What is it?"

I wrecked my brain trying to figure out something to say. I don't really know why I wouldn't allow myself to tell people about the box and the note. It just seems too personal to talk about. Even with my new supposed family.

"Kassey, we are here to help you. We want you to be comfortable here." Hayley reached out towards me and I drew back.

"Why didn't you just leave me out there?" I suddenly asked.

Even in the dark, I saw hurt cross her face. "I would never do that."

"Everyone always wants to. I don't belong here. Why did you even want to take me in? You have plenty of kids here. Why was I needed?" I pressed.

"Well, you needed a good family. You've been hurt too many times, Kassey. I can see that in your face. I can see it in the way you walk, in the way you look at others, and in the way you talk. You are afraid to commit. You are afraid to get close to people because someone has burned you before. I can't say I know how it feels, but I know how to prevent it from happening again. You won't have to worry about that here."

Hayley grabbed my hand before I could move away. It wasn't a firm grab. It was the type of motherly touch. The touch Alice would always give me when I felt hurt or upset. It was the type of touch I vaguely remembered my mother giving me. It was meant to comfort.

"You don't need to keep running away. You belong here. You may not see that now, but you will soon. I want to be your home. I want you to feel safe and loved in a way you need and never had. I want to be your mother."

"I already have a mother." I snatched my hands away.

"I didn't mean it like that, Kassey. I meant… I want to be someone you can feel close to and someone who you can look up to." Hayley kissed my cheek and smiled tiredly at me.

I turned and headed toward the door. I meant to leave, but I stopped. Hayley muttered in her sleep. I couldn't tell exactly what she said, but it sounded like she said, "I love you."

I didn't want to go to school the next day, but I made myself go. Jason was quiet the whole ride there. I could tell he was still upset about yesterday, but I couldn't make myself form the words to apologize. When Cameron stopped the car, Jason jumped out and speed walked towards the school. I sighed and walked in with Cam.

Before we split up, Cameron turned to me. "Jason told me what happened yesterday."

"And you hate me, too." I said sourly.

"I don't hate you, Kassey. Jason's upset. He does a lot to make people happy and doesn't understand when people throw it back in his face."

I flinch. "I threw nothing in his face."

"You need to do something. There was no reason to run away. I know Hayley talked to you, but she wouldn't tell us what about."

At least there's one trustworthy person here. "Cameron, I'm trying, Ok? I didn't mean to hurt Jason."

"Why did you?" He challenged me.

"I don't know. It's a reflex. I'll..I'll try to make it up to him." I said, thinking.

"You better." The bell sounded and Cameron walked off.

*   *   *   *

I slammed my things down on my desk in psychology class and Evan jumped back.

"Damn, who did you kill?" He joked.

"Shut up." I said and buried my head.

He tilted his head. "What's wrong?"

"I did something stupid and now I don't know how to fix it." I muttered.

"You want to know what I do when I mess up?" He started.

"What?" I lifted my head a little.

He smiled. "If it's with a niña, I buy the biggest bouquet I can find and dance for her. If it's a niño, then I buy him something shiny and give them my car for a week or throw them a partido. I am the master of grande fiestas." Evan made a little dancing gesture, and I laughed. I liked the way he rolled his tongue when he said some words in Spanish.

"Are you serious?"

"Hell yeah. You don't know how many times I have messed up and how many times I have become broke from messing up." Evan complained.

I burst out laughing and Evan told me to shut up before we got in trouble. I didn't know what it was about him, but I always forgot why I was upset when I was around him for a while. He always knew how to make me happy, even when I didn't want to be.

"So, what was your mess up?" Evan asked me.

The feeling of dread returned. "I yelled at someone and I didn't know how upset he was."

"You hurt his feelings?"

"I didn't mean to! I do stupid things when I'm mad. I just wanted to be alone." I explained.

"What happened? People don't just explode for no reason." Evan pressed.

I sat there frozen for a moment. Did I want to tell him?

"Kassey." Evan waved his hand in front of my face.

I blinked. "What?"

"Are you going to answer or…?"

"If I tell you, promise me you won't say anything." I said sharply.

"It's nothing illegal, is it?" He asked, while slowly leaning back.

"No," I took a deep breath, "I have a note from my parents that I keep somewhere to refer to from time to time. I also have a little box with things that are important to me. Yesterday after school, I came back to find them missing." My voice got lower as I talked.

"And you freaked out." Evan added.

I nodded. "So, I kinda tore the house up, and I yelled at Jason in front of everyone because he wanted to help, but I wanted to be alone to look."

"I get it. Though, yelling at him *in front* of everyone may have not been the best thing to do." He said, shrugging.

"I know. I didn't even know I hurt him until today. I didn't mean to. Jason's been nice to me."

"Sometimes it's easier to be meaner to those who are the nicest to us. We know they care and we know they will still be there. It's normal." He told me.

"You always support everything I say, even when it's bad." I observed.

"Well, I know you're not a bad person. You may just make poor decisions. Trust me, I can't be one to judge." Evan responded.

I nodded. I was kinda glad I told someone. Even though I didn't really say the whole truth, I could feel lighter without all the stress. We didn't really talk that much through the rest of class. Before Mr. Holden ended class, he assigned us a project.

We were to present a PowerPoint or poster of the brain's functions and how they affect the body's movements. We could work with partners or groups of three. Only that. Everyone packed up, and I did as well. I really didn't want to do anything that had to do with school and thinking, but I needed to pass the class.

"Kassey."

I turned my head to look at Evan who was looking at me with an uncomfortable expression. "Yeah?"

"Do you want to be partners?"

"Yeah. You may have to help me. I haven't been in this class for that long." I said sheepishly.

"No problem. We'll do it at my place." Evan said while still packing up.

"Your place?" The nervousness from before came back.

"Would you prefer your place?" Evan looked at me from the corner of his eye.

I thought about Evan coming over to the Johnson's house and him never really leaving. "Nope. Your place is fine." I blurted.

Evan smiled. "You got a phone?"

I nodded and handed it to him, then he handed me his. After we exchanged numbers, he grabbed his backpack and slung it over his shoulder.

"I'll text you later, sí?" Evan asked me as he walked out.

"Ok." I nodded and watched him as he left.

*   *   *   *

I got to my second to last class of the day, Spanish, in a daze. Our teacher, who we call Señorita Lucía , was at the front of the classroom writing some words and sentences on the chalkboard. I sat down in my seat at the back of the class. Spanish was a class that I was both failing and passing. I didn't even know how that was possible, but Spanish wasn't exactly my strong suit. I took Spanish because I thought it would be an easy language to learn. I was sadly mistaken.

"Kassey, did you do the homework?" My friend Emily asked me quietly.

"Nope. I forgot we even had homework." I whispered back.

Emily rolled her eyes, but nodded. Turns out, no one in the class did the homework, so Lucía gave us another day to do it.

My last class was gym. They called me out of Spanish yesterday, so I didn't get the chance to go. Someone had reported yelling and having seen confrontation yesterday in the parking lot. I quickly told them there was nothing that happened. I knew I shouldn't have lied, but I couldn't tell them what happened that day. I would not snitch, no matter how strong the feeling was to do so. I kept my mouth shut. But, when I left the office, I thought I saw Khalil's smiling face through the door's glass, prideful and taunting.

I changed into my gym clothes as soon as I got inside the locker room. I changed from my outfit and into a pair of white workout jeggings and a red crop top that had lines of black on the sides. I actually liked gym. Running and being physical were some things that I liked to do that calmed me down. I remembered when I was younger and I would run with my parents in the morning during their workouts.

"Come on, Kassey. You can do it." My mom looked behind her at me as we ran down the street.

I struggled to keep up with them, and I stopped to catch my breath. "Mommy...my chest hurts."

My parents stopped and jogged back to me. My mother kneeled down to my height and looked me in the eye. "Kassey, you can do anything you put your mind to."

"But...I can't, mommy. You and daddy run too fast...I get tired." I said, putting my head down.

My mom lifted my head up with her finger. I saw my dad kneel next to my mom. "You are our little angel. We will always help you reach your dreams. You may be too young right now to keep up with us, but you will be able to someday. You just need to keep trying." My father had said.

"I can?"

"Of course you can. Kassey, you are beautiful and smart. There isn't anything you can't do." My mother kissed my cheek and gave me a bright smile, which I returned.

They both stood up. "You ready to keep going?" My mother asked.

"Yeah!"

*   *   *   *

I blinked to find myself back in the locker room. My parents had disappeared and the smell of my mother's perfume had changed to the smell of gym clothes and shampoo from the shower. I sighed and went to join the rest of the class.

It didn't seem like too much time had gone by. People were just doing random exercises in the gym. I looked at the group of people until I found familiar faces. I walked up to one, and he looked at me with surprise.

"Kassey." It wasn't exactly a question, but Evan seemed thrilled to see me.

"I didn't know you would be in this class." I said, looking around at everyone else.

"Same here. Nice outfit." He said while looking me over.

I blushed. "T-thanks."

"...I guess I'm not the only person who thinks so." Evan looked behind me.

When I turned around, I saw some guys crowded together, glancing at me and smiling when I met their eyes.

"Hey, it's—what's wrong?" Evan's face stopped me from saying much. His face seemed to show anger and his eyes glared daggers at the boys until they got the hint and scurried away.

"Nada. Nada." Evan turned away from me.

I didn't buy it. "Evan, what's wrong?"

He sighed. "I hate it when guys do that. It's gross. We're still in school and they still do it." Evan scoffs.

"Well, I don't care. I'm not looking at them." I responded calmly.

Evan's face was blank for a moment before slowly changing into a smile. I was glad I could cheer him up. The moment his expression had changed, I had wrecked my brain to figure out how to calm him down. I didn't like the feeling that I felt from him. I figured Evan was a person with a bad temper that he just didn't show around me. It showed itself in his off moments when he thought no one was watching.

Today was a free day, so Evan and I spent the next hour and a half playing basketball. It was another thing that I enjoyed doing. My dad would take me to the basketball court and watch me as I struggled to make a basket, and celebrate when I finally did.

"Look daddy! I did it!" I screamed as I jumped up and down.

My father smiled down at me and picked me up. "Yes, you did! I'm so proud of you, Kassey! I knew you could do it!"

I giggled. "Will we always do this?"

"As much as you want to." My dad's eyes lit up when I had asked him. He always loved doing things with me you would normally do with a son. I just made it easier for us to connect that way because I enjoyed many things a boy would. I just wanted to hang out with my dad.

My dad smiled at me and ruffled up my hair.

*　　*　　*　　*

I sighed as I closed my gym locker. I didn't want to go home. I knew I would have to face Jason when I went outside to the parking lot. Avoiding him would not work anymore and him trying to avoid me was getting uncomfortable. I needed to fix this *before* we got into the car with Cam. I walked out of the locker room to see Evan waiting at the door. I almost didn't see him until he fell into step with me. I stopped and tilted my head at him, which he responded with an idiotic smile.

"What?" He asked innocently.

"You waited here for me?"

"What else do I have to do?" He shrugged and continued walking.

I followed next to him. "Don't know. I just don't like making people wait on me."

Evan stopped so fast that I had to trip myself so I wouldn't run into him.

"You know, the whole time I knew you, I noticed you weren't like anyone I have ever met." He started.

"Is that a good thing?" I asked worriedly.

"Yeah. It's a great thing. I just don't know what kind of difference it is. You're really quiet when you want to be, and you're really guarded. Why?" He looked at me seriously.

I hesitated. "Isn't everyone guarded from time to time?" I usually answered a question with a question when I wanted to avoid answering.

Evan stared at me for a moment. "Sí...sometimes."

"Kassey!"

I turned around when I heard someone yell my name. Cameron ran down the hallway and stopped when he reached us. He looked between me and Evan.

"What?"

"We need to get going. I have to pick up the girls, remember?" He sounded irritated.

"Right," I turned to Evan, "I have to go."

He nodded at me. "I get it. I'll text you later, ok?" He nodded to Cameron and walked away.

"Who was that?" Cameron asked me as he watched Evan leave.

"He's a friend. I met him yesterday in psychology and today in the gym." I didn't know how much Brianna told him, but I didn't want to mention the lunch.

"A friend?" Cameron smiled.

"Yes, Cameron! A friend! Can we go now?" I asked, and started heading for the car.

I heard Cameron laugh behind me. I rolled my eyes and kept walking outside to where Jason was waiting for us. When he saw me, he glanced away. I sighed, and we all got into the car.

Jason ran right to his room when we got to the house. I watched him go upstairs and contemplated whether I should follow him before deciding that it would be a good idea.

I knocked on his door and listened to the sound of his bed shuffling as he moved. He opened the door, then tried closing it once he saw it was me.

I pushed my arm against the wood. "We need to talk."

"There isn't anything to talk about." He pushed harder.

I grunted. This boy was stronger than he looked. "Please, Jason—Ow!" The door closed on my hand as hard as it could. I ground my teeth together to keep from screaming. The pain made me madder than him crushing my finger.

"You ok?" Jason swung the door open and gently took my hand to examine it.

"Not really." I watched him but he didn't pay me any mind.

Jason took me to the bathroom and took care of my hand. "Good thing Hayley has things for practically every injury." He said as he rummaged through the cabinets.

"Jason." I said as he wrapped up my hand, which had turned bright red and purple in some spots. Jason had said it was fine because it would heal while bandaged.

"Yeah?" He didn't look at me while he tried to fix my hand.

"I'm sorry. I didn't mean to yell at you. I didn't mean to hurt your feelings. I didn't know I did."

"Why did you? You never *think* before you do things, Kassey. You hurt everyone who tries to be nice to you." Jason whipped his head around and looked at me with a sad face.

"I didn't mean to. I don't know how to….I don't know how to accept someone caring for me that way." My voice broke. I willed myself not to cry.

"Let me help you, then. I want you to feel like I can be your brother. I don't want you to push me away. It hurts when you do. Please let me show you that other people can care for you just the same." Jason's eyes bored into mine.

"You don't hate me?"

"I could never hate you. It just hurt to see you like that and to have it taken out on me. It wasn't fair." Jason explained.

"I know it wasn't fair, and I'm sorry. I just wasn't in the mood for conversation. I never meant to speak that way toward you when you've been nothing but nice to me. You didn't deserve it." I wasn't much for admitting I was wrong, but I meant it. I didn't know I upset Jason, and it hurt me to know that he felt that way because I had a sharp tongue.

"It's alright. We just have to work on that. Ok?" Jason asked me.

"Yeah." Jason helped me stand, and we both walked out of the bathroom.

I made my way to Jade's room and knocked on the door. She looked at me and motioned for me to come in.

I reached into my pocket and handed her the necklace. "I can't take this."

"Why not?" She asked, confused.

"It seems too personal. I couldn't ask you to hand over something so nice and...I just couldn't take this from you." I explained.

"You're not taking it, Kassey. I gave it to you. I want you to have it. That's why I gave it to you." Jade giggled.

"Oh..Ok." I said, frowning.

"It's nice for you to care about that, though, but, Kassey, it's ok to accept nice things from someone else without having to give anything in return. It's called a 'gift.'" Jade said sarcastically.

"I know what a gift is, smart alec." I shot back.

Jade laughed and shook her head. When I left her room, my phone buzzed. I looked at the screen to see that Evan had texted me to let me know he was ready and if I needed to be picked up. In my pursuit of making sure Jason was ok, I forgot I was meeting up with Evan. I ran into my room and found my bookbag. I stuffed it with my Spanish work and a few meaningless things for no reason. When I tried to hurry downstairs, I tripped on the second to last step and stumbled to the floor.

"Woah, what was that?" Hayley looked up from the TV when I tried to play off my embarrassment.

"Nad–nothing." I hurried to the kitchen.

Hayley followed me. "Why were you running?"

I sighed. "So, this...guy, Evan, is picking me up so we can study for this project at his house, and I completely forgot about it." I quickly explained.

"A boy?" Hayley's voice had the same tone Cameron's did when he asked about Evan before.

"Oh, my god, yes. A boy. We are *studying*! Nothing else."

"Uh-huh. Yeah, sure." Hayley smiled at me. She moved as if to leave, then turned back around. "What happened to your hand?"

"Um, nothing." I didn't look at her. Hayley stared at me for a moment before going back into the living room.

I groaned and tried to find a snack and gave up when I came up empty. Maybe I'll ask to stop by the store or a market on the way there. The doorbell rang and Hayley went to get it. I heard Evan's voice, and I waited behind the kitchen counter until they finished talking. The boy smiled at me as Hayley let him inside.

"Pleasant home, Mrs. Johnson." Evan remarked.

"Thank you." Hayley smiled at her.

"Kassey, how long have you've been living here? This place is mucho grande." Evan said, looking around.

Hayley responded before I could. "Not very long. She's been here for a few days since I took her in. The kids took a liking to her quickly." She giggled.

I stiffened. Evan's face took on a look of confusion as he glanced at me, but I didn't acknowledge him. I didn't understand how these people could talk about their and other's personal business so openly!

"Are you ready?" I asked him hurriedly.

"Y-yeah. Um, nice meeting you, Mrs. Johnson." Evan said as he followed me out.

"You, too. Be safe, you two!" Hayley yelled as we left.

"Kassey! Kassey, slow down!" Evan yelled as we got outside. I ran as fast as I could to the car.

"What?"

"Why are you moving so fast?" Evan asked as we reached his car.

"No reason." I said too quickly. Evan gave me a look.

We drove to his house in silence. He pulled into the driveway of a really friendly house that looked like they recently repainted it. It was a brick house, and the bricks were very visible despite the fresh paint. The house was dark on the outside but gave off a welcoming feeling when we pulled into the driveway. Evan killed the engine and sat there.

"What did she mean by 'I took her in?'" Evan asked me after moments of silence.

"Nothing. She meant nothing." I stared out the windshield.

"Kassey, look at me." He demanded.

I did. "What?"

"What did she mean? It looked like it made you upset."

"Does it matter?"

"If you're keeping secrets from me, yes. It does." Evan said angrily.

"I'm a foster child! Ok! Is that what you want to hear?" I yelled. It tore me up to admit it out loud, but he would not let it go, and I hated keeping things from Evan.

He blinked at me. It seemed like he didn't know what to say, and that made me feel worse.

I scoffed. "Yeah, I thought so." I got out of the car and started walking away from the house.

"Wait! Wait." He caught up to me and blocked my path. "Please wait."

"Why? It's not like you would want to have anything to do with me now." I shrugged.

"I didn't say that...I-I just wasn't expecting you to say…" He trailed off.

"Why? Is it because I'm not like you? I absolutely *despise* telling people I am a foster child because of the exact reaction you just gave me. They treat me differently. They think I'm fragile or have a disease or something foreign. I never really acknowledged it out loud to anyone." I admitted.

"I get it. I mean, I won't treat you differently. I think it's brave that you told me."

"Not that you gave me any choice." I shot at him.

Evan sighed. "I'm sorry. I don't do really well with boundaries sometimes. Really, Kassey, it doesn't matter if you have an extra toe or were born with two heads. I still see you as the 'suffer in silence' girl I met yesterday in psychology class." Evan smiled at me.

I laughed even though I didn't want to. I still hated the fact that I told him, but I liked the fact that he was willing to see it differently than other people would. I just hoped nothing changes that.

Evan took me to his room, and we worked on the project. Evan's room had a musical vibe. There weren't any posters, but he had a guitar in the corner next to his bed and a stack of papers on his nightstand on the other side of his bed. Evan's bed cover showed musical notes that spread from top to bottom. I sat on the bed and looked at Evan as he worked to clean up his room.

"Sorry. I didn't really have time to clean up." He said as he picked up some books.

"It's fine. Your room isn't really that messy. Do you play?" I asked, pointing to the guitar.

He looked up and nodded. "Yeah, in my off time. It's the only thing I know how to play. I can't sing." He chuckled.

"Hmm..."

"Is there anything you know how to do? Do you play or sing? I know you know how to play basketball." Evan sat down next to me.

"Yeah. I used to play with my dad. I would also sing with my mom. She loved to sing and I would join her." I said sadly.

"You miss them, don't you?" He asked softly.

"You have no idea." I cleared my throat. "Ok, um, do you want to start or…?"

"Yeah, paper or technology?"

"Paper. Definitely paper."

Evan gathered a poster board and pencils for us to start the project and he told me to search up some facts about each brain function.

"What happened to your hand?" He asked me as I started writing.

"My brother slammed my hand into the door by accident when I was trying to apologise."

He inhaled sharply. "Wow. That's rough. Are you alright? Did you guys make up?"

"Yeah, we did. My hand will heal. Ok, you said that the heart doesn't need the brain to function."

"That can be a fun fact. We need functions that the brain has that help the body. How about...the left side of the brain helps with speech and language while the right side helps with visual and processing information?" Evan suggested.

"Why do you need me again?" I said as I rolled my eyes.

Evan laughed. "I didn't want to do this alone. Plus, you got this. I need help."

"Yeah right." I snickered, but kept searching for things.

Evan and I laughed the whole time. We barely finished the project before we got extremely bored. Evan kept asking things about me and I tried my best to answer his questions, even when they made me feel uncomfortable.

"You don't have to tell me if you don't want to. I get it if it's too personal." Evan shrugged.

"I don't mean to be so secretive. I just want to keep things to myself that belong to me, if that even makes any sense." I shook my head.

"It does. You don't want anyone prying. There is a thing called 'privacy' and it isn't illegal." He joked.

I scoffed. "Yeah, well. My parents left when I was about 3 or 3 and a half, almost 4. I don't really know why they wouldn't take me with them. They wouldn't tell me what was wrong."

"Have you heard from them since then?" He tilted his head.

"No, I don't have a way of contacting them. I want to go find them when I turn 18 and when I'm legally out of the system. I do not know how, but I have three years to figure that out." I said, then groaned. *Three years!*

"I'd be happy to help you find them now." Evan said, sitting up.

"What?" I looked at him sharply. What did he mean?

"One thing no one knows about me: I'm a damn good hacker. Not even my parents know, because I would surely not have a phone or computer anymore." He explained.

"You hack?"

"I'm fantastic at finding out information. If you even want my help." Evan stared at me.

"Are you kidding me? Of course, I want your help! Why didn't you say something before?!" I punched him.

"Ow! Because I didn't think it mattered to you." He rubbed his arm.

"Well, I want your help. Please!"

"Ok, ok. Calm down, Kassey. I told you I would do anything you wanted." A smile showed itself on his face. "Look, after we're finished, I'll see what I can do, Ok?" He promised.

"Yeah. That's cool. Thanks." I smiled back. I would finally find out something about my parents! I don't think I even remembered being this happy in a long time since my parents left.

"You hungry, or are you going to pretend you ate something before you left?" Evan asked me.

How did this boy know me so well? "I'm hungry."

He laughed. "I know a place that makes great gelato." Evan jumped up, then stopped to turn around and face me. "You like gelato, right?"

I shrugged. "I never had it."

His face dropped. "What?"

"I never had that. I've had water ice?" What the hell was gelato?

"*Dios mío*. You hurt me sometimes, Kassey. What have you been eating all your life?" Evan frowned at me.

"What is gelato?" I ignored the fact that he spoke in Spanish.

"It's basically frozen yogurt. You want to go or do you want to rummage in the kitchen?" Evan asked, sounding impatient.

"We can go." I grabbed my bag and followed Evan out of the door.

*   *   *   *

"Do you live by yourself?" I asked as we were on the road.

"Nope, I have a brother, sister, and live with my parents. They all went out of town last week." Evan explained.

"Wait, they left you here? For over a week?" I asked him, shocked.

"Yep." His voice sounded bleak.

"Why? I hardly find that fair." I retorted.

"Well, I'm the *alborotador*. The bad seed in the family. Plus, I'm the youngest. They said they wanted a peaceful vacation for a few weeks." He shrugged.

"When are they coming back?"

"I don't know. They didn't say, but you know what?" Evan looked at me before facing the road again.

"What?"

"I'm kinda glad I didn't go. If I did, I wouldn't have met you."

I felt my face get hot, but I didn't acknowledge it. Getting ice cream suddenly sounded fantastic. We drove the rest of the way in silence. Evan drove me to an ice cream shop, and he said he was determined to get me a gelato so he could say he was the first to get me to eat one. I rolled my eyes, but I was genuinely interested.

We walked up and got in the long line. I don't think I have ever seen a line as long as the one we stood in now. It was both a fascination and an irritation.

Evan saw my face. "What's wrong?"

"Do you always do this?" I point to the line.

"Not always, but yeah. It's not normally this bad when I come." He angled his head toward the front.

"How much money do you spend?" I asked, remembering the lunch and now this.

"Not as much as you think. The guy at the grill gives me a discount for me doing whatever he wants. Plus, I always have stashes of cash somewhere." He whispered the last part. I raised an eyebrow at him, and he laughed. "I love it when you do that!"

We got to the front and Evan ordered two strawberry gelatos. He gave me one, and he watched me as I ate it. "Wow." That was all I could say.

"Is that a good 'wow,' or…?"

"It's good. It's great." I said, sounding surprised. When I watched them make it, it horrified me at the thought of having to eat one.

"Yay!" Evan devoured his ice cream and waited for me to finish before we headed to the car.

"Where are we going?" I asked him as I looked at the clock. It was almost six.

"I know you may have to get back, but I want to take you somewhere first." Evan said.

"Where?"

"It's a surprise. I'm sure you'll like it." He said confidently.

I looked out the window and watched the trees fly by us as we sped down the road. It seemed like we weren't in Baytonwood anymore, and I really confirmed it when I saw a sign that said we were leaving town.

"Where are we going?" I turned to him.

A crooked smile showed itself on Evan's face. I tilted my head, but knew he would not tell me. *This boy is weird*, I thought. Moments later, Evan took me to a place of trees, bushes, flowers, and shrubs. He pulled into the grass and turned off the car.

"We are in the middle of nowhere, Evan." I complained.

"Not really. Trust me, Kassey. You will have fun." He promised.

Evan and I went hiking through the woods. I had never been hiking before and I knew I sucked at it, but Evan didn't complain. He helped me regain my balance from time to time and he pointed out a few animals that we came across. I actually had fun.

"What's your favorite animal?" I asked as we walked.

"My favorite animal would be a wolf."

"A wolf?"

"Yeah. Wolves take authority and they do whatever they have to in order to survive. I respect that. Also, people take advantage of them. I feel bad for them sometimes." Evan explained. "What's your favorite animal?"

"Either a husky or a blue jay." I responded as I rubbed my hands along tree bark.

"So you like blue."

"I like blue, yes, but I like Crimson more. I also like lynxes." I turned my head to see Evan looking at me. "What?"

"Why don't you like letting people in?" He suddenly asked.

"Because it helps nothing." I answered calmly.

"You're afraid of commitment. Why are you so sure that people will hurt you?" Evan put his hands in his pockets and waited for me to answer.

"Every time I open up to people, I get let down, and they get taken from me. Some of those people made me wish I didn't show them who I was." I stared at the ground as I talked.

"You can't keep hiding yourself, Kassey. There are people who you can trust. You just have to find them." Evan stepped closer to me and took my hand in his. "You don't have to be afraid anymore. You'll see that not everything about the world is horrible." He kissed my hand, and I smiled. I was actually enjoying being here with Evan. It took my mind off of things and he made me happy.

Evan and I kept hiking until the sky turned dark. I couldn't see as we tried to retrace our steps back to the car. Evan turned on the flashlight on his phone as we walked. I stopped and looked up at the sky for a moment.

Evan looked back when he realized I had stopped. "What's wrong?" He walked up to me.

"Nighttime is beautiful." There was a full moon tonight. It was my favorite moon because of the fables of supernatural stories my parents would tell me.

Evan looked up at the sky. I couldn't see his face clearly, but I could tell he was thinking. "Yeah, the moon is full. It always makes the sky look brighter than it's supposed to be." He responded.

I adjusted myself to get a look at his face. The light luminated enough to show a thoughtful and concentrated expression. I could see the longness of his eyelashes and the sparkle of his brown eyes as he looked at the sky. His hands moved to his pockets as he gently rocked back and forth on his heels. Evan didn't notice me staring at him until I crept from the tree. His head angled toward me, and I could no longer see his face clearly. I kept walking toward him and he waited until we were face to face with each other. Evan moved one hand and placed it on my cheek, making me lean into his touch. His hand was warm, and it felt good on my cold skin.

"Close your eyes." He breathed.

I slowly closed my eyes, and for a moment, nothing happened. As I was wondering what he was doing, I felt his lips on mine. They lingered, hungry and wanting, but also hesitant. I responded slowly so as not seem desperate, but I was taken aback when he kissed me. I didn't expect him to respond to me that way. Did he feel something for me, or was this a "in the moment" thing?

Evan gently backed us against a tree and deepened the kiss. His lips moved to my neck, and I leaned my head back. My body became warmer, and it felt like electrical currents were moving through my veins. I gasped as everything suddenly looked clearer. Evan moved down my shoulder, then back to my mouth.

"Evan...Evan..." I stopped and touched my forehead to his.

We sat there panting. Everything around us seemed to stand still. My body felt like it was on vibrate. I had never kissed a boy before and enjoyed it.

"What? Why did you stop?" He asked breathlessly.

I gave him a quick kiss, which he quickly responded to. Evan wrapped his arms around my waist and I tangled my hands in his hair. Evan pulled me closer to him and we slowly attacked each other. I forgot where I was, I forgot that it was dark outside and that we were surrounded by animals and twigs, I forgot the fact that I was supposed to be scared about putting myself out there with anyone. My mind was wild and wired with excitement and exploration, but then, we ended up on the ground. I had slipped on a loose part of the mulch below the tree and took Evan with me.

We laid there laughing for a while. "I am such a klutz." I said, chuckling.

"It's fine. I think that was the universe trying to tell us something."

"Tell us what?" I propped myself up on my elbows.

"That we don't want to do anything we might regret." He stared at the sky.

"You regret what happened?" I could hear the hurt in my voice.

He did, too. He quickly sat up. "No, I don't regret what happened. Not at all. I meant that we wouldn't want to take it too far. I know we kinda just met, and I don't want to make you feel a certain way." He explained.

"I loved it, Evan. I don't regret it either." I crawled to him and gave him a kiss on his cheek. I saw a shadow of Evan's hand raise to touch his cheek and I imagined a smile on his face.

"Are you ready to go?" Evan asked me as he stood up.

"Not really." I muttered. I didn't want this moment to end. I still felt the effects of his kiss and my body still felt like it was electric. I had never felt this way, and I wanted to hold on to it for as long as I could, but before we got into the car, my phone buzzed repeatedly. I reached into my pocket and got blinded by the light as I turned it on. The phone screen was filled with messages and phone calls from Cameron, Hayley, and Jason. How did they get my number?

Hayley: "Where the hell are you? Answer your phone!"

Hayley: "Kassey, I am tired of these games. I know you are out with Evan, but you are still supposed to check your phone!"

Cameron: "Kassey, please answer your phone. Mom's getting worried. We are all worried. Please text me back."

Hayley: "Kassey, if I don't hear from you in the next five minutes, I am calling the police. You better answer the phone! Now!"

Cameron: "Kassey, I don't know what you are doing or where you are, but this is really freaking people out. Did you lose your phone? Please text us or call us. Hayley's pacing and keeping us all awake until you come back. She's also threatening to call the police, but Jason and I are trying to dissuade her from doing that. Please tell us where you are. We are worried. We love you."

4 missed calls from Hayley.

2 missed calls from Cameron.

5 missed calls from Jason.

It was almost eleven o'clock. I cursed under my breath. I really messed up. I didn't even hear my phone ring and I never really thought to check what time it was. I told Evan what happened, and he sped us back to the house. When we pulled up in the driveway, I jumped out of the car. All the lights in the house were on.

He rolled down the window. "Do you want me to come in? I can help explain what happened."

"No, I think that will make things worse. Plus, I don't want you getting blasted. I'll see you at school tomorrow, okay?" I said hurriedly.

Evan nodded and drove off. I turned towards the house and ran inside.

It was bright when I opened the door and I could feel the tension in the house. I knew I was in for something. I closed the door and walked into the living room and faced five angry and worried faces.

"I can explain."

"Where the hell were you?! Do you know how worried we all were?!" Hayley screamed.

"Hayley–"

"We thought something happened to you! You didn't call or text!"

"I didn't hear my phone, and I didn't get the texts–"

"You could've told us you were going to be late, Kassey." Jason chimed in.

"Well, I didn't know–"

"Where were you? What were you doing that was so important that you couldn't even bother to send a small text?" Hayley asked bitterly.

I said nothing. Hayley rolled her eyes and scoffed. Jade and Aliyah looked at everyone with tired expressions.

"Say something!"

"Quit yelling! I don't have to tell you a damn thing! I'm sorry I made you worry, but you don't have to know everything I do!" I yelled back.

"I am your mother–"

"You are not my mother! Don't you ever say that! You will never be my mother!" I felt my temper flare. How could she even say that to me?

"Kassey, you can't talk to her like that." Cameron said slowly.

"You're right. I can't. I'm sorry that I hurt your feelings and I'm sorry for not doing what I was told. I wanted to hang out with a friend and it ran over a little late. Sorry I have such a crappy phone and I couldn't text you the *juicy* details!" I retorted.

I saw Jason flinch, and I immediately felt bad for upsetting him again. Aliyah started crying, and that made me feel worse. I ran up to my room and slammed the door.

CHAPTER THIRTEEN

Morning came and I was laying there staring at the ceiling. I didn't even want to acknowledge the fact that the fight happened. I knew I hurt a lot of feelings, but I also didn't care. I had school today, but I didn't want to go. I would have to get in the car with everyone and I didn't know how they felt. I decided I would skip today, and that was the reason I was still in bed.

My phone buzzed, and I reached under my pillow.

Evan: "¿Dónde estás?"

Me: What?

Evan: Sorry, I forgot. Where are you?

Me: "I will not be there today."

Evan: "Why not? Are you sick?"

Me: "I had a fight with everyone last night and I couldn't sit in a car with them for seven or ten minutes there and back."

Incoming call: Evan.

"Yes?" My voice sounded irritated.

"Are you ok? I kinda had a feeling something bad would happen." His voice sounded muffled.

"Well, yeah. You were right. They immediately started yelling at me and I couldn't even get a decent word in." I explained, remembering how Hayley had cut me off many times.

"Did things get better?" I heard screams and the sound of a stampede in the background.

"Nope. By the time I could say a full sentence, I was already angry, and I fought with them. I said stupid things."

"Uh-oh."

"Yeah."

"What are you doing?"

"I'm counting how many cracks and peels there are from the chipped paint on the ceiling of my bedroom." I said with fake curiosity.

"Get dressed. I'm picking you up." I could hear the sounds of voices in the background fade and be replaced with wind.

"I can't ask you to skip." I sat up.

"No one said you asked me to. This is a good excuse for me to get out of this hellhole." I heard his car engine start. He was serious.

"Where would we be going?"

"That's for me to know and you to never figure out."

I laughed and told him I would be ready. Evan gave me an estimated time of ten minutes. I ran, jumped into the shower, and quickly got dressed in my black ripped jeans and a blue cropped mini top. I went into my closet for my black leather jacket and quickly put it on. I reached for my phone and made sure the ringer was on before putting it in my back pants pocket. I looked at myself in the mirror and decided I looked decent. Before I went downstairs, I made myself look in one of my dresser drawers. Ever since I lost my things, I would check every day to see if they would turn up. So far, they have remained missing. I closed one eye and opened the drawer to see a folded up piece of paper. My heart started racing in my chest. I quickly grabbed the paper and unfolded it to see my mother's handwriting. The note! But how? I ran to look under my bed and found the box there, too. What the hell was going on? Why are my things suddenly appearing like they were never lost? I put the note in the box and I raced downstairs.

I smelled the aroma of breakfast as I descended the stairs. Hayley was in the kitchen with her back turned to me. I could hear music coming from the TV, so she didn't hear me come down. I walked over to the counter that was directly behind her. I bit my lip as I tried to figure out what to say.

Hayley turned around and jumped when she saw me. "Kassey. Wow, you scared me. How long have you been standing there?"

"Not long." My voice was a near whisper.

There was silence. "Kassey—"

"Listen, I'm sorry for last night. I didn't mean to say all of that."

"You were right. I can be pushy, but you know that...after what happened to you before..I become afraid when I don't hear from you. I think that something happened to you and that I lost a child. I never like to think that way." Hayley explained.

"I understand."

"Also, I could never replace your mother and I never would want to. I know that's a sensitive topic for you and I crossed a line last night that I would never cross. Emotions ran high, and we all said things we regret." Hayley continued.

"You're right. I'm sorry."

Hayley nodded. "Why aren't you in school?"

"I can't face them after that. I said a lot and I don't know how they all feel. I think it's better if I don't go today." I said, shrugging.

"You can't skip, Kassey." Hayley disagreed.

"Well, I won't be alone, so you don't have to worry." I hoped she wouldn't ask anything further about that.

She didn't. I think she already knew who I was referring to. Her face showed it. Instead, she said, "Did you find what you were looking for that day?"

"Kinda. They just showed themselves in my room, why?" I tilted my head at her.

Hayley shrugged. "Just wondering."

I stared at her for a moment. "Were you the one who took them?"

Hayley said nothing. She just went back to cooking. I watched her as I slowly put things together.

"Hayley, answer me."

She turned to me. "Yes?"

"Were you the one who took my things that day?" I asked her slowly.

She licked her lips and nodded. I shook my head. Oh, my god! And I thought she was the most trustworthy?! She walked into the room that day, knowing why I was a wreck, and gave me that speech about wanting to make me feel comfortable and loved here. She was the reason that day happened in the first place! She was the reason Jason and I were on the outs!

"Oh, my god. I can't believe you."

"Kassey, I have a reason."

"Let me guess: you were cleaning my room? You were curious that there was a shiny blue box under my bed and you wanted to know what was in my sock drawer? You stole those things from me and said nothing!" I yelled at her.

"I didn't know what they meant—"

"Why were you even in my room?!"

"My husband wanted to know more about you. I knew how guarded you were and I wanted to find out for myself. I realize now that I may have overstepped some boundaries." She tried to explain.

"*May have?!* Hayley, those things mean *everything* to me. My heart broke into *pieces* when I saw they were gone! I wasn't just upset. You gave me that fake speech about how I will be welcomed and loved into this family while you knew you were lying to me!" I screamed.

Hayley's face showed hurt. She lowered her head and wiped her eyes. I wouldn't allow myself to feel sorry for her. My pride and anger wouldn't let me. I wanted her to know how much I hurt that day. I wanted her to feel the loss and pain I felt. The helplessness and despair I felt. I wanted her to know exactly what I went through and see if she still wanted to help me.

The doorbell rang, and I went to open the door for Evan. I walked outside and Evan quickly turned and ran to match my pace as we reached the car. We didn't talk until we were well away from the house.

"What's wrong?"

"What makes you think something's wrong?" I stared out the window.

"You seemed like you couldn't wait to leave that house. Plus, you don't seem thrilled. Are you still upset about last night?" Evan asked sensibly.

I took a deep breath. "Remember when I told you I blew up at Jason, my brother, when I lost something important to me?" I started then suddenly realized that I called Jason my brother.

"Yeah?"

"Well, I just found out this morning that Hayley took them." I said meekly.

"Who's Hayley?"

"My foster mother." I answered absently.

"Wow...and you blew up?"

"Of course I did! She went into my room, took my things, and said nothing. She stood there, looked me in my face, and didn't say a word. She let me wallow and she talked about wanting me to feel like part of the family and opening up to everyone, while knowing damn well she was the reason we were in that situation in the first place!" I rambled.

Evan waited till I was finished. "Wow...um...I don't know what to say."

"Well, thank you for helping me find a distraction and getting out of the house. I really need it." I went back to looking out the window.

"No problemo. Is there anywhere you want to go?" Evan asked.

I thought for a moment. "I want to go to the beach."

Evan started laughing. "Alright. Beach, here we come."

We rode for a while until we found ourselves on Tybee Island. It was a long, long drive, but I was so excited to see the waves crash against the shore and to see people in bikinis and surfing. The air smelled like salt and the sounds of screaming children and water filled my ears. I hadn't been to the beach in a long time. Evan found us a pleasant spot near the water, but not so close to the other people.

"It's ironic that I had a towel in the trunk for us to use." He said as he sat everything on the towel when he found a spot. We both lay on the towel and watched people run back and forth through the sand and watched the seagulls try to eat the food people dropped.

"So, why did you pick the beach?" Evan asked.

"It's peaceful and wasn't in Baytonwood. I wanted to get away for a while. I feel like I made things worse from last night between Hayley and I." I spoke absently.

"That was mostly my fault. I was supposed to have you back, and I neglected to watch the time." Evan took blame.

"No, we both messed up, but I'm not ashamed of it. I don't wish that last night didn't happen. I just wish it didn't end in a fight." I said sadly.

Evan moved closer to me and took my hands in his. "We aren't here to make ourselves depressed. We are here to have fun. We may not have bathing suits, but that doesn't mean we can't still go swimming." Evan smiled at me.

I giggled, and we ran toward the waves. We splashed each other and gagged on salt water. It was so much fun, and when we left, we were soaked in water and hoping that the sun would dry us off. We walked on the boardwalk and took part in the games. Evan brought us food and snacks to eat as we walked. I now stood near a little food store that I had never heard about because Evan said he wanted to try them. He seemed to know the things on the menu, so I let him order. When he came back, he held something that looked like a kabob, and I gave him a look.

"Just try it. Please?" He inched it closer to me.

I hesitated for a moment before biting it. It was the worst thing I had ever tasted!

Evan saw my face and gave me a sheepish look. "See—d-don't get mad…"

"What was that?" I scrunched up my face.

"I wanted to see your reaction to meat."

"Why?"

"Maybe you were lying." He shrugged.

"Well, that was no reason to poison me." I said, annoyed, and spit it out.

"Sorry. I won't do that again." Evan gave me a small smile.

"I made you upset, didn't I?" I sighed.

"Not really. I just want to know more about you. I don't think I really know you all that well."

"You know things about me."

"Not intimately." Evan muttered.

"What do you want to know?" I tilted my head at him.

"When were you born? What's your favorite thing to do?" He asked as we started heading towards the car.

"I was born February 20, 1997. I like to Read, draw, sing, run, and play basketball." I answered him.

"You're very talented."

"Thanks. When is your birthday? What do you like to do?" I turned to look at him.

"I was born December 7, 1997. I like to play my guitar and hang with you." He moved his foot and crossed his arms.

I lowered my eyes. "I'm not that interesting. Only that we have the same birth year."

"Not that many girls can play basketball and sing. It's kinda hard. Do you dance?"

"Nope. I can't dance." I laughed to myself, remembering me trying and failing epically. "You know other girls who can sing and play ball?" I raised an eyebrow.

"I'll teach you." He promised, ignoring my question.

I slowly shook my head. "You know how to dance?"

"Yeah, why are you looking at me like that?"

"I didn't know you knew how to dance...and you completely ignored my question."

"I am a hombre of many talents." He puffed out his chest, and I laughed. "As well as the question, that isn't really that important. I don't know many people, not many girls. I have all guy friends. It doesn't really matter that much." Evan shrugged. I just watched him and didn't say anything, but I made a mental note. I felt like there was something he wasn't saying. Not necessarily lying, but there wasn't much truth to his answer. It gave me an uneasy feeling, but I didn't want to invite problems to a good moment.

Evan dropped me off at the Johnson's house at about 4:18pm. I knew everyone was home by now and I wasn't looking forward to seeing them, but I knew I couldn't avoid them every time we had a squabble. I was just tired of being the one trying to fix things.

I took the steps two at a time until I reached Jason's room. He was the one I wanted to start with. I knocked on his door, but he didn't answer. I thought he may be asleep, but I really needed to talk to him. I opened the door and stood there frozen as I watched my brothers kiss.

Chapter Fourteen

"Oh, my god."

They both looked at me and horror crossed their faces. I couldn't stop looking at them. Weren't they related? Cameron walked quickly behind me to close the door and lock it.

"Kassey—"

"What...ah—what?" I stuttered.

"C-calm down. Please." Jason said, sounding scared.

"We can explain." Cameron said quickly.

"Yes. Please. Explain." I said each word as one syllable.

"Well–"

"Aren't you related?" I blurted out.

They stared at me. "No." Cameron dragged the word out.

"We've been good friends for a long time—years really—and got adopted together. Look, I know this is bad—"

"So you guys...are dating or…?" I looked between them.

"Please don't say anything. No one knows." Jason pleaded.

"No one is going to, right?" Cameron glared daggers at me, but I refused to shrink away.

"I'm not a snitch. I would not say anything. I just—I never had this much of an awkward situation to walk in on." I said, looking around the room to avoid staring at them. The air in the room felt tight and hard to breathe.

"You're not upset, are you?" Jason asked.

"Upset? Why would I be upset? I'm kinda confused and very baffled." I rambled, then mentally chastised myself for showing how unnerved I was.

"Why are you even in here?" Cameron growled.

"I-I wanted to apologize for last night. I didn't know if you were still mad, so I wanted to talk to you guys about it so we don't go back to hating each other." I slowly explained as my mind tried to unscramble itself. I had totally forgotten why I had come.

"Well, I don't hate you. You know I can't." Jason smiled at me.

I smiled back and looked over at Cameron. He had crossed his arms and was looking at the wall. Jason tilted his head at him and frowned. Well, I guess I was back on Cam's naughty list.

I went to my room and sat on my bed. Today has been a long day, I thought. My head was spinning as I thought about what I had just walked into. What the hell was that? Good thing is that they weren't related. Bad thing is that they were adopted together. It was against the rules, per se, if you date a sibling they fostered you with. I always noticed how close they were, but I didn't know it was like *that*. I would never say anything to anyone about it, but I just hoped no one else walks in on them like I did.

*   *   *   *

Cameron started acting towards me the same way he did when I first came. I worried we went completely backwards and we would never get back to where we were because of one confrontation. Jason had tried to reassure me he was just afraid of what I would do.

"He didn't expect you to walk in. Neither of us did." Jason had said sheepishly.

"Well, I told him I wouldn't say anything. It's not my place." I shrugged.

"Well, Cameron's a person who's kinda hard to make certain once he thinks a specific thing." Jason sighed.

"I promise you. I won't say anything." I nodded to him.

My phone buzzed in my pocket. Emily had been texting me nonstop. She and Brianna wanted me to come by the mall to do some shopping with them. Shopping was not my favorite thing in the world to do.

Emily: "Come to the mall with us! You need some time out!"

Emily: "You can't ignore me forever!"

Emily: "Pick up the damn phone, Kassey!"

Me: "What do you want, Emily?"

Emily: "Finally! Me and Bri are at the mall and she's been bugging me about having you come here with us! Please say you will come."

Me: "You know I hate shopping."

Emily: "Please! Please! Please! Please! Please! Please!"

Me: "Fine! Ok! I will go if you promise to stop saying 'please.' Ok?"

Emily: "Yay! Text me when you're ready to be picked up!"

I groaned. How do I always get myself in situations I don't want to be in? I went downstairs with everyone when Hayley called us for dinner. Hayley and I's relationship hasn't really gotten better since I found out she took my things. I haven't talked to her since I left the house this morning and dinner was a quiet event. It seemed to be wrong if anyone said anything, so we ate in silence. After dinner, I texted Emily so she could pick me up from the house.

I was in my room when there was a knock on my door. I looked up and saw Jade standing in the doorway. I waved her in and sat on my bed. Her face had a serious expression, and I was afraid to know what was on her mind.

"Where are you going?"

"I'm meeting with a few friends." I said as I got myself together.

"Who?" She asked as she slowly came into the room.

"Why does it matter to you?" I said firmly.

She glared at me. "I can't know where my sister is going?"

"I just don't think it really concerns you, Jade." I said, shrugging.

She scoffs. "Look, everything is falling apart! Hayley's upset at you, Cameron is mad and irritated, and Jason is trying to fix everything again, while me and Aliyah are stuck in the middle as usual!" She yelled.

"What do you want me to do about it?"

"Try telling them to suck it up!" Jade said with a squeal.

"Make things worse? Nope. Sorry, kid." I frowned at her.

Jade sighed. "Do you really want to be here or are you tolerating us because they brought you here?"

"I am trying to get along with everyone here. I promise you that."

My phone buzzed with a text from Emily telling me she was outside. I walked past Jade and went downstairs. Jason watched me fly down the stairs and looked as if he wanted to tell me something.

"What?" I asked him.

He opened his mouth, then closed it, and shook his head. I squinted at him, then shrugged and left the house. Emily's face brightened when I got into the car and she sped to the mall.

"Brianna would not shut up until I could tell her for sure that you were coming." She explained.

"Where is she?" I looked around the car, seeing only Emily and I.

"I left her there. She's waiting for us. We are starving and there are some things we wanted to show you at the mall. There were so many sales and so many guys who wanted to sell things to us." She rattled, then giggled at the end.

I rolled my eyes. She was exactly like Bri, a guy magnet. That was all they seemed to care about. It was kinda sad, but hilarious at the same time. We got to the mall and Brianna was waiting for us at the entrance after we parked the car and walked up to her.

"There you are! You are such a hard person to get a hold of!" She complained.

I clicked my tongue."I've heard."

"We have so much to show you." She dragged me inside.

The mall was packed with people. That was another reason I hated shopping. There were too many people you had to deal with. Sales made people competitive and crowds made people rushy and impatient. Emily and Brianna brought me to several stores and had me try on several outfits. Most of them made me look ridiculous, but some were ones I actually liked. They figured out my style because Brianna's expression would change whenever I went to a specific selection she had been avoiding.

"You like gothic?"

"Not exactly gothic. Just black." I answered while searching through the clothes.

"You had to have known her style, Bri. Look what she has on." Emily chimed in. The way she said it sounded a little snarky. Brianna scrunched up her face and still tried to steer my attention elsewhere.

We were at the mall for hours. We bought some clothes, tried some samples, and watched people bicker over prices of clothes and try to figure out who had what first. It was funny to watch other people's problems because it made you forget about your own. I think they were trying to get me in good spirits with this trip. When it was lunchtime, we found ourselves a table and sat down.

"So, how do you feel?" Emily asked me.

"I still hate shopping, but this was kinda eventful." I admitted.

"You can't ever be bored with me!" Brianna sang.

Emily rolled her eyes, and I giggled. I asked if they were hungry and we all decided that we were in the mood for Mexican food. I went up to one of the side restaurants and placed an order. As I waited, my phone went off, and I checked it to see several texts.

Hayley: "Where are you?"

Hayley: "I know you're mad at me still, but please don't start this again, Kassey."

Jason: "I'm sorry you felt like you had to run away from us. We don't mean to make you feel that way. I hope I didn't just break the trust I felt we had. Please tell me you don't hate me, Kassey."

Jason: "We all love you, Kassey."

Evan: "What are you doing?"

I answered Jason, telling him I didn't hate him, and I still trusted him, and answered Evan, telling him I was at the mall with my friends.

Evan: "Then what's with the big frown?"

Me: "What?"

Evan: "Turn around."

I looked up to see a very familiar-looking boy with his phone half covering his face. I scoffed and waved him over. I couldn't risk losing my spot while waiting for the food.

"We have to stop meeting like this." He joked.

I rolled my eyes. "Are you following me?"

"Well, I just had the strongest craving for the 2 for one sale." Evan said sarcastically.

"Evan, as much as I love seeing you here, I don't want you anywhere near Brianna."

"Who?"

I motioned towards the girls, and Evan followed my line of vision. Emily caught his glance and smiled. Evan turned back and gave me a half smile.

"So, who's Brianna?"

"My friend with the red highlights. The one who loves the attention you don't want to give her." I said, sighing.

Evan laughed. "Well, good thing I'm a lady's man."

I tilted my head at him, but didn't question it. They called my name for the food and Evan dragged me back toward the table after I got myself situated. Brianna watched us as we drew near and her eyes followed Evan as he came around the table.

"My name's Eván. May we sit?" He asked.

"Sure. Yeah." Emily said, giving me a look in the corner of her eye. She mouthed, "Manners," to me and I rolled my eyes.

Evan pulled up a chair from another table and sat down next to Emily. I took my seat next to Brianna. She winked at me, and I responded with a small groan.

"So, Evan, how did you know to be here?" Brianna started.

"Excuse me?" He looked confused.

"She means 'how did you know we would be here?'" I clarified.

"Oh," Evan shrugged, "Well, I was actually here with a couple of guys. They like to hang out in the food court and go through the sports and shoe stores." He explained.

"Why didn't you say that before?" I asked.

"I enjoy messing with you." He laughed.

Emily looked at me and her mouth formed a little "O" as she gave me a, "What does he mean by that?" look. I shook my head and gave her a, "Mind your own business," look.

"Well, I've heard you two went to lunch at the beginning of the week. How was that? Where did you go?" Brianna fished.

Evan's eyes glanced at me once. "Um, a Mongolian grill that's a few minutes from the school. I've become a regular there."

"The lunch was very interesting." I added.

Evan shook his head at me. I didn't want to put anything in Brianna's head anymore than he did. I hoped that our answers would be a hint to her that she should drop the subject.

She didn't. "How did you guys meet?"

"Can you please drop it, Brianna?" I asked, glaring at her.

"What? I'm just curious." She shrugged at me.

"You're always curious." I muttered. Brianna scoffed and turned away. Evan cleared his throat and leaned back in his chair. I stole a quick glance and saw Emily trying to get Evan's attention with her hands. She would slide her hands up his arms, but he would slowly move around in the chair, as if he was trying to escape her without standing up. I heard a small giggle escape from Em and saw her hand reach lower before a little annoyance passed through Evan's face.

"Tengo que ir." He stood up.

"What?" Bianna looked at him, confused.

"I gotta go." He quickly clarified, keeping his attention on the ground.

"Already?" Emily frowned at him.

"Yeah, the guys are probably waiting for me." Evan looked at me.

"Um, are you guys done?" I grabbed their trash and walked away from the table without waiting for an answer.

Evan followed. "I was worried that you weren't one to take hints."

"I've learned to see hints even when there aren't any." I sighed.

Evan looked me over. "Are you ok?"

"I'm spectacular." I said sarcastically.

"I know that voice and that face. Go ahead and vent. Tell me all you need to." He put his hands in his pockets and waited.

"Didn't you have to get back to your friends?"

"They can wait. I'm sure they haven't noticed that I've been away for a while." Evan smiled at me.

I opened my mouth, then closed it. As much as I wanted to vent to Evan, I couldn't. I didn't really see what good it would do me. Besides, what could I say that wouldn't incriminate me or anyone else?

I decided not to say anything about myself. "You didn't come with friends, did you?"

"I did. Honestly, but, you're right. It's not the entire reason I wanted to find you and talk." He admitted.

"What is the reason, then?"

"I did some looking, and I found some things you may be interested in."

"What? What did you find?" I asked excitedly.

"I didn't exactly bring it with me because it was kinda bad, but they're at my place." He sighed.

"What do you mean by 'kinda bad?'" I asked suspiciously.

"Like, legal bad…" He drawled out.

"Can I look at them?" I was almost afraid of seeing what he found. Legal stuff?

"Um, I kinda rode with my guys, so I don't have my car. If you stay here, then I can swing back or just pick you up from your house." Evan suggested.

"House may be better. I have some amends to make." I sighed. I had a few people I needed to talk to.

Evan nodded. "Well, I'll see you later, ok? I'll text you." He said as he started walking away.

"Bye and thanks!" I waved at him.

CHAPTER FIFTEEN

I asked Emily to drive me back home. After saying goodbye to the girls, I climbed out of the car and headed inside to be met with warm air. Everyone was in the living room or outside in the backyard. I went out to the backyard and Aliyah squealed when she saw me. Her tiny figure raced toward me and I picked her up.

"Hey, little one." I smiled at her.

"You finally picked me up!" She yelled happily.

"Don't get your hopes up, kid." I put her back down.

Aliyah giggled, and I watched as she ran back to her toys. I heard a tap on the screen door behind me and turned to see Cameron standing behind the glass. When our eyes met, he nodded and motioned for me to come inside. When I followed him into the kitchen, Cameron's back was facing me. I sat on the counter and watched him until he talked.

"Where did you go after dinner?" He asked quietly.

"I went to the mall." I said, then shrugging.

Cameron gave me a half smile. "The mall? You don't seem like the shopping type."

"I absolutely hate shopping, but I got dragged into it." I sighed.

Cameron chuckled for a bit before becoming serious again. "Look, about before, I'm not mad at you."

"Then why did you act like you despised me *again*?" I crossed my arms.

"I don't despise you. I was just really on edge and messed up from what happened. I wasn't expecting you to be there." He explained.

"So, explain it to me. I really don't understand…Cam, you have to know well enough by now that I don't tell other people's personal business." I said firmly.

He nodded. "Yeah. I know that. Um, Jason and I are in a complicated situation, you could say. Um, we met about a year or two ago as friends--foster friends. Then we got separated and then reunited. The second time we reunited, we kinda...got together. I know you're not supposed to when you're adopted together, but...I don't know. It just happened." Cameron sounded very uncomfortable.

"So, you were afraid you would get caught and be separated again." I guessed.

"Yeah. They would surely send us to different homes, and I didn't want that to happen."

"So, be more careful next time. You know, people like Hayley will just walk in like I did. Try locking the door or...putting up a, 'Do not disturb' sign." I playfully punched his shoulder.

Cameron snickered and ruffled my hair, which I responded to with a glare. My relationship with Cam seemed to be one that was on and off if there was one thing that we didn't agree with.

"You and Hayley need to talk." Cameron suddenly said.

"What? No." I shook my head.

"Kassey, you and her have been on the outs for a while now. You can't try to live in the same house and hate each other at the same time. It doesn't work that way." Cameron stared at me.

"What did she say was the reason we weren't talking? Hm?" I demanded.

"She did something wrong and disrespectful and didn't tell you about it." He responded coolly.

I scoffed. "That's all she said?"

"Well, you tell me then. What did she do that was so bad?"

I was quiet for a moment. I really needed to learn when to bite my tongue. "She took something my parents gave me and didn't tell me about it. She also gave me a talk about loyalty and trust and about how she wants me to feel loved and secure here with everyone. The whole time she was lying to me." I explained.

"Maybe she wasn't lying about the talk."

"Maybe not, but she still should've told me she took my things instead of letting me run around the house an insane wreck!" I barked.

"Yeah, I agree with that, but you two need to talk and stop fighting. It's going to get annoying. I promise you that."

"I'll try, but I can't promise things will take a miraculous turn for the better." I said, shrugging.

"I know. I just want you to *try*. That's all I ask."

I sighed and asked Cameron where Hayley would be. He told me to try her room, and a few minutes later, I was looking at Hayley's closed bedroom door. I wasn't nervous, I just didn't know how to feel about me trying to fix our relationship into a more healthy family relationship. I closed my eyes and knocked on the door. I waited for a while before hearing a faint, "come in."

Hayley's face showed surprise when I walked into her room. "Kassey. Hey. What brings you here?"

"Um, can we talk?" I felt so uncomfortable standing there looking at her.

"Yeah, sure." Hayley motioned towards the bed, and I shook my head.

"I can stand. Um, about before with the whole, 'box and possessions,' thing..." I started.

"I was way out of line and I know I overstepped in so many places. I owe you a lot of apologies and I promise you I won't do anything like that again. The kids here aren't that big on me walking in their room, so I assumed you were the same. I should've come to you first." Hayley interrupted.

I stood there looking at her. I didn't expect an immediate apology. "Um, thanks. I was really mad, and I snapped and I'm sorry. I need to learn how to think before I do things."

"You don't owe me an apology. You have every right to get mad, though you *do* need to think before you act. We both have some things we need to work on. Again, I promise you I won't do what I did anymore." Hayley smiled at me.

"So, are we ok?"

"Yes, we are ok, Kassey." My foster mother pulled me into a hug before I could reject it. I grunted but didn't pull away because I knew the effort would be a waste. My phone started ringing, and I finally pulled away from Hayley and left the room to answer it.

"Hello?"

"Hey, are you ready?" Evan asked me. I heard wind in the background.

"Yeah, I'm ready. Just knock on the door. Everyone is mostly outside." I told him as I went back downstairs.

"So, do you want me to go to the backyard? I'm right around the corner." The sounds of the wind changed to the sound of the engine idling.

"Yeah. That's ok. I'll meet you outside."

"Cool." He hung up.

Cameron was still in the kitchen and he turned when I came down the stairs. I tried to keep my face as blank as I could so he wouldn't ask anything I didn't want to answer.

"So, how did things go with Hayley?"

"They went better than I thought it would. She actually started out as soon as I got there. She told me how sorry she was and how wrong the whole situation was. I really did not know what to say after that." I shook my head as I finished talking.

Cameron smiled. "Well, that's a good thing. No more fighting between you two."

I heard loud voices in the backyard and Cam and I went out to see what the commotion was about. I saw the kids, Jason, and Evan crowded together. I opened the screen door and Evan's face brightened when he saw me.

"Hey." I said when I walked over to him.

"Hey." He responded as Aliyah ran squealing to the two of us.

"Hello! I'm Aliyah! What's your name?" She asked him.

"Um, hey, kid. I'm Eván." He gave her the strangest and most uncomfortable look that I burst out laughing.

"Hi, Evan. Kassey has talked about you a lot." Jade said as she sat on the ground trying to match colored blocks.

"Really?" Evan winked at me.

"No, I didn't, Jade. Mind your own business." I snapped.

Jade smiled and shrugged at me. "Fine, be like that. I only speak the truth."

I rolled my eyes. "Can we go now?" I asked him irritatedly.

Evan never lost his smile. "Yeah, we c—"

"Hold up. Not so fast." Cameron came up to us.

"Great." I muttered.

"Yeah?" Evan stared at him.

"I know I've seen you around, but if you're going to be hanging around with my sister this much, we need to talk." He stated.

"No, we don't, Cam." I dismissed it.

"Yes, we do." He crossed his arms, and we both stared each other down.

"Fine." I caved when my eyes watered. Cameron nodded and he, Jason, Evan, and I went into the playroom.

"So, what is this talk about? Cool room, by the way." Evan asked as we got ourselves settled in the playroom. He looked around in amazement at everything that was in the room.

"Thank you. I want to know what business you have with Kassey." Cameron asked.

"Well, she's a very interesting person who has a hard time fitting in places. I just want to be the friend she needs. Plus, I enjoy hanging with her." Evan explained easily.

"Good answer." I whispered to him. Evan responded with a smile.

"So, you will not be those people who always get her into unnecessary trouble, are you? She can already do that on her own." Jason asked serenely.

"Hey!" I hissed at him.

Jason shrugged, but Evan shook his head. "I won't get her into trouble. I'll take care of her. Lo prometo." He said, putting his hand over his heart.

Cameron gave him a look, but nodded. "Alright. Whatever. Just don't be late like last time, alright? Check your phone, Kassey." He demanded.

"I will. Don't worry." I pulled out my phone and checked it in front of them just to show I was serious.

Cam and Jason left to go back to the backyard, and Evan and I stayed in the playroom for a bit.

"Wow. That was like an interrogation from two dads." Evan pretended to wipe away sweat.

"Did you mean what you said? And what language did you speak?" I asked, remembering that the words he ended with weren't English.

"Yes, I meant what I said, and it was Spanish. Didn't you notice what my last name was?" He tilted his head at me.

"Revera. Yeah." I recalled Brianna mentioning it once.

"Yeah. My parents are proud of the last name we have. I could care less about it." Evan sighed.

"You mean, 'couldn't care less,' right?" I corrected him. Evan gave me a look that said, "Don't correct me," so I left it alone. "Do you want to go? I really want to see what you found." I was suddenly eager to get out of the house.

"Oh, yeah. Come on." Evan grabbed my hand and we headed outside.

CHAPTER SIXTEEN

Evan brought me to his room and immediately went looking through his drawers. I stopped and looked around his room again. It had a welcoming feeling that you felt when you walked inside. Everything about the room was musical: the bed, the walls, the instruments. Evan was a musician at heart.

"Found them." Evan pulled out papers and news articles and placed them on the bed. We both went through the piles of papers and read them to ourselves. I picked up one that seemed interesting. It was a brief excerpt from a newspaper that seemed to have been torn up.

"January 18, 1989. Police arrested a man and woman today at 3:48pm. Their house was searched, and they found many suspicious substances. The couple were handcuffed and arrested. No one knows the charges and supposedly, they are heading towards the police station as we speak."

Another paper was a list of bills and card information Evan wrote to show how their money was spent.

^Item: 2 Passports ^Item: utility bill ^Item: Post bail

^Money spent: $250 ^Money spent: $200 ^Money spent: $23,000

^Date: Feb. 16, 1989 ^Date: Nov. 22, 1985 ^Date: Feb. 18, 1989

^Where: private ^Where: private ^Where: BDC

There was a little more on the bill, but what really struck me was the location of "BDC." What was that? I asked Evan what that meant and he said it stood for, "Baytonwood Detention Center." Was that jail? How could they buy passports if they were incarcerated? Did someone else buy them for them? Why would they try to leave and why did they spend so much money on so many things? I suddenly wanted to stop looking at the papers in front of me, but I willed myself to keep going. I picked up another article and read.

"Police raided a man and woman's home on December 1, 2000. They found the house bare and abandoned. They assumed the couple had skipped town a few hours or minutes before. Police also reported finding a four-year-old girl lying on the floor in her room. Officials sent the child to the hospital and later put the little girl into the foster care system. Police wondered why the parents left their child alone at home in such a condition."

Another paper was notes and descriptions from the hospital.

"Name: Kassey Conwell

Age: 4

Physical Description: Brown hair, black eyes with flecks of auburn, small body, slim fingers, calloused palms, bruised face, bruised arms, and bruised neck.

Height: 38.5"

Weight: 32.0lb

Notes: Kassey was found, according to police, on the floor unconscious and not breathing. She seemed to have had a

panic attack. She has a troublesome medical history of asthma, night terrors, and is very low in height and weight. She also seemed to have a history of panic attacks and migraines. Kassey is an underdeveloped child who seems to have not been taken care of as much as she should've been. We have given her morphine and are waiting for a response.

Checked by: Doctor Griffin"

I stared at those papers in utter shock. W-what? Was that what happened to me after they left? I didn't exactly remember it, but I didn't know I landed in the hospital and had that many problems. Was that how I ended up in the system? Is that why I was always being prescribed those medications I stopped taking a few months ago? I always wondered why I always had so many things going on with me as I grew up. There was so much about my past that I just didn't know. I realized I had been clutching the papers in a death grip and Evan was staring at me.

"Are you ok?" He asked quietly.

"How did you find these?" I whispered.

"I did some research online and found some old newspapers and things. I thought that was what you wanted." He spoke slowly.

"I wanted you to find out all you could about my family. I just didn't expect...all of this." I dropped the papers and covered my face as I sat on the floor.

It was quiet for a moment before Evan spoke. "What are you thinking?"

"Are my parents criminals?" I was almost afraid to ask, but I wanted to know the answer.

"From what I found, they aren't angels. They usually work together to get different substances and sell them off for profits. It seems to have been going on for a while." Evan explained.

"Since when?"

"1989." Evan was still watching me.

I scoffed. "So, my dad was 16 and my mom was 13."

"It's been a long time. They never really got caught that much until your mom had you." Evan added.

I turned to him sharply. "Are you saying that this is all my fault?"

"No! That's not what I'm saying at all! Look, your parents started getting caught after 1989, but they had to look after you when you were born, so they kept trying to be careful and they made more mistakes that way. You being born actually troubled things for them, so little of their work actually got done. You actually helped to slow things down." He tried to reassure me.

"That makes me feel worse. My birth was my parent's downfall." I said bitterly.

"Don't see it that way. Besides, now you know more than you knew before." Evan tried to cheer up the conversation.

"Did you at least find out where they were?" I asked him hopefully.

"Um, I tried to. I looked up BDC and they have a firewall that I can't really get through yet, but I'm trying. I think I found something else, though. It might be somewhere in this pile of papers." Evan searched through the papers on the floor, then handed me some to look at.

"What are these?" I asked him while looking at each of the pages.

"They are information on phone bills, medical bills, and house bills. I traced the credit card number to find an address, but all I found was an offshore account name." He said sadly.

"What name?" I asked curiously.

"Samson Hart. I also found out that the account was set up by phone. So, I traced the phone, and the address is only a few hours from here."

"Let's go! We can talk to Samson and ask him what he has to do with my parents!" I started getting excited.

"Don't get your hopes up just yet. That doesn't mean he has all the answers. It's only an address and name, which may not even be a real name." Evan told me.

"That's all we have, Evan. It's worth a try to see if he has anything we can use. Please." I pleaded.

Evan looked at me like I was slowly killing him. He sighed and nodded. Evan told me we would go in a couple of days because his parents were coming back and he needed to get a few things straight. As he dropped me off at the house, I turned back towards the car and Evan rolled down the window.

"Um, thanks for all the things you did for me. You didn't have to spend all your time researching and looking for pointless articles."

"No problemo. Plus, it wasn't pointless if it meant a lot to you. I would gladly do anything for you if it makes you happy and content." He smiled at me, then added, "I also called the doctor, Giffin, who examined you when you were young."

"What did you find out?" I leaned on the window.

"They couldn't exactly give out any confidential information, but when you were brought in, you were in critical condition. You were covered in bruises, and part of your skin was swollen. They tried to wake you up, but you wouldn't wake, and that was why they gave you morphine. They thought you had a history of abuse of something." He explained further.

I thanked him, turned away, and headed toward the house. Evan called my name, and I turned back just in time to hear the slam of his car door and see him running towards me.

"What's wro—" Evan quickly pulled me towards him and kissed me.

He put his hand behind my head and deepened the kiss. Before I could even fully comprehend the situation, the kiss ended and Evan backed away with a small smile on his face.

"I needed something to hold on to. See you in a few days." He said before turning on his heel and walking away.

CHAPTER SEVENTEEN

I've been living with the Johnson's for half a year now. I arrived at the Johnson's house May 22, 2011. It is now November 19, 2011. I've developed a better relationship with everyone here and I've even come to enjoy being here. I haven't been adopted yet, but Hayley had asked me if I wanted to be adopted and become a Johnson.

"You want me to be a Johnson?" I had asked her uneasily.

"Only if you want to. You've been here long enough to know much about us, and I wanted to know if you wanted to make it official. You don't have to if you don't feel ready yet." She explained.

I didn't know what stopped me from saying yes. I felt comfortable with the family, but adopting myself into the family seemed to be going too far. Maybe in the future, I may let myself consider it, but right now, I'll stick to living with them and keeping my last name.

Another good thing, Evan and I had grown closer in the past couple of months. He was going to introduce me to his family today since they got back from their vacation a few months ago. Evan also wanted to have me meet his friends since they kept asking him because he always talked about me to them, and he wanted to take me to the address he found before so we could get another lead on my parents. Evan had asked me to be his girlfriend as well in July and that was when we started hanging out more. Cameron, Jason, and Hayley have been asking about us since they found out I had a boyfriend.

"So, when can we talk to him?" Hayley had asked.

"You guys already met him." I shook my head at them.

"We met him as a friend. Now, the conversation is different, Kassey." Cameron had said not letting up.

I sighed, but knew I wouldn't win the argument. Evan and I had a lot to get through in the next couple of days. Evan was going to pick me up soon so we could go to his house for a little while and then we would go find the address Evan had written for me as a lead.

My phone began ringing, and I had to run around my room to find it. "Hello?" I said breathlessly.

"Hey, you alright?" Evan's voice was filled with concern.

"Um, yeah. I couldn't find my phone, but I could hear the annoying ringtone I meant to change." I rolled my eyes.

Evan laughed. "Wow, my ringtone's annoying. Says a lot about the relationship." He joked.

"Shut up." I smiled to myself.

"Alright," He said slowly, "I'll be pulling up in a few minutes. I just thought you would want to know."

"Thanks. I'll be ready." I hung up. I turned to go downstairs, but stopped myself and looked at my bed where the box was. I pulled out the box and looked for the note to read my mother's handwriting, like I had done so many times before. I stroked my fingers over the paper as if any hard strokes would tear it apart.

"Happy birthday, Dad." I whispered to myself before putting everything back and heading downstairs.

*   *   *   *

Everyone looked at me when I came into the kitchen. I stopped and stared back at them. I still hated being the center of attention. What had I done this time?

"Why are you looking at me like that?" I asked them.

"No reason. You just look really ready to go somewhere." Hayley fished.

"Huh, nice try. I already told you guys I was meeting his family today, so you can't say you knew nothing." I went around to the fridge.

"Just don't do anything stupid." Jason suggested.

I looked at him, annoyed, with a cup of orange juice in my hand. "Thanks?" I said sarcastically.

Jason shrugged, and then the doorbell rang. I let Cam get to the door and stayed behind the counter, waiting for Evan to come inside. He and Cameron shook hands and smiled at each other as he came inside. His smile grew bigger when he saw me.

"Hey." He said as he came over.

"Mmm, Hey. They may want to talk to you before we leave." I whispered to him, remembering the conversation I had with them before.

"Should I be worried?" He whispered back.

"What are you two whispering about?" Cameron called to us.

"I'm just telling him the prep work to prepare for a Johnson interrogation." I said, shrugging.

Jason and Hayley rolled their eyes, but Evan clapped his hands together. "I am ready for the questions. Bring it on!" He said readily.

I spent an uncomfortable ten minutes listening to everyone fire questions at Evan and him answering them with informality and occasionally having to rethink his answers to not say the wrong thing.

"Can this interrogation be over?" I interrupted the conversation when it turned towards backgrounds.

"Kassey, we aren't finished—"

"I'm finished. Let's go." I was really eager to find out all I could about my parents since we were so close. The only downside was that I had to go through Evan's parents to do so. When they let us leave, Evan drove us to his house. I saw another car in the driveway that was the color of a blue jay. Evan parked beside his parent's car and took the keys out of the ignition. He leaned back in his chair and closed his eyes as he sighed.

"What's wrong?"

"I didn't tell you this...my parents don't speak a lot of English." Evan confessed.

I blinked at him. "W-what?"

"Don't worry. My siblings do...and my parents speak a little." He tried to clean it up.

"So, what you're saying is that I'm screwed." I sighed.

"How much Spanish do you know?" He asked, sounding hopeful.

"Probably not enough…" I answered sheepishly.

"It's alright. I already told them you were coming and that you may not understand them. My siblings know enough English to understand. They're very excited to meet you, which makes me nervous." Evan gave me a half smile before getting out of the car and coming around to help me out.

We walked into the house, and the air seemed to be different. I could feel that the house was full, and that there were more personalities here than just Evan's musical and bad boy vibe. This house now seemed to have a calm and family-like manner.

"*¡Mamá!*" Evan yelled as he went into the kitchen.

I got the chance to look around the living room since I never really stopped to explore the house before. There were pictures of Evan and his siblings, as well as his parents, on the mantle above their fireplace. Their furniture of couches and loveseats were violet cream colored. All the floors downstairs were wood and the floors upstairs were carpet. When I heard voices coming toward me, I turned to see Evan coming back into the room, followed by his family. While looking at them, I wished I had paid more attention in Spanish class. Evan whispered something to his parents before walking over to me.

"So, um, this is my sister, Elena, and my brother, Nicholás." He pointed to his siblings, who were sitting on the couch. "My parents are Isabella and Isaac." He pointed to his parents, who were sitting on the loveseat. They were all looking at us, and it was making me feel very uncomfortable.

"What did you tell them about me?" I asked him.

"¿Cómo se llama?" His mother asked.

"She wants to know what your name is." Evan translated.

"Oh, um, me llamo Kassey. ¿Cómo estás?" I responded slowly. I knew most of the introductions. Anything else that required a lot of pronunciations was where I got an F-. Evan looked at me with such surprise that I wanted to laugh, but I kept it inside. His parents and siblings looked impressed.

"Bien. Encantado de conocerle." His mother replied with a smile.

"She said that it's nice to meet you." Evan told me.

"Is this the girlfriend you were telling us about, Hermano?" Evan's sister said in English. She had the same accent as Evan did when we first met. His brother probably did, too.

Evan chuckled. "Yes, she's the girlfriend."

"No entiendo." Isaac said, looking confused.

"Mamá, papá, te presento a Kassey. Esta es la novia de la que te estaba hablando." Evan told them.

Evan's parents looked at me strangely before finally smiling, well his mom smiled. Evan's dad didn't exactly seem happy. Isabella came to hug me and I stood there immobilized and not knowing what to do or what Evan had said.

"Um, w-what's going on?" I stuttered.

"I told them we were dating and my mom acted like that was the magic words or something." He looks at his mom with a face of discontent.

His mother seemed to feel my discomfort because she backed away and gave me a look of almost guilt. "Lo siento." She said.

"She said 'I'm sorry.'" Evan translated.

"No. Soy vale." I said slowly and gave her a small smile, which she returned. After a few more questions and translations, Evan finally told them we had to leave.

"Do you have to leave now, Eván?" His sister, Elena, asked.

"Yeah, we have somewhere to be." He started getting a bag ready and started stuffing papers and snacks into it.

His brother gave him a look. "Where are you going, Hermano?"

"Don't worry about it, Nicholás." Evan said defensively. Nicholás squinted his eyes at his brother, but said nothing more.

"Um, Encantado de conocerle, Familia Revera." I waved to them as Evan pulled us out the door.

"Come visit sometime, Kassey!" Elena yelled.

"¡Adiós!" Evan's father yelled. I haven't heard him speak one word to me the whole time I was here.

"That was the most Spanish I've spoken in my life...Evan, wait! Stop!" I yanked my hand out of his and stopped running.

"What?" He said as he turned to face me.

"Why are you running?" He seemed to be in such a hurry to get away from the house.

"We have somewhere to be. I thought you would want to be there as fast as you could." He spoke fast.

"Evan, you're running away." I told him.

He sighed. "I told you that my relationship with my family isn't that great."

"They seem fine." I said, looking back at the house.

"My parents are fake. I fight with them all the time and my siblings are stuck in the middle. All they do is take the side of whoever they think will win." Evan explained angrily.

"Don't worry too much, Evan. You'll get wrinkles." I patted his cheek and got into the car. I saw Evan shake his head but turn to follow me into the car. He put the keys into the ignition and we got onto the road.

CHAPTER EIGHTEEN

It took hours, many roads, and many highways, until Evan was sure he knew where the house was. The houses in the neighborhood were kinda beat down. It gave you a certain vibe that made you want to turn around and leave. Evan pulled up to a house that had broken windows upstairs and downstairs, the paint on the house was peeling, and had broken porch lights. I looked at the building from the car and suddenly didn't want to get out.

"You're shaking." Evan said as he shut off the car.

"What?" I quickly turned to him and the sudden movement caused everything to spin for a minute.

"Are you ok?"

"Yeah, I just...I just have a headache." Me saying that reminded me of the hospital note I looked at saying I had migraines.

"Are you sure you want to do this?" Evan asked me.

I took a deep breath and thought for a moment. I needed to do this. If I want this bad enough, I will get myself together and get out of this car to get the answers I want.

"I'm ready. I want to do this." I said confidently. Evan nodded to me and we both got out of the car.

Evan knocked on the door, and we waited. At first, we thought the house was abandoned, but Evan said he heard movement inside of the house. The door opened to show a middle-aged man with tired blue eyes and a wrinkled face. He stared at us for a moment before really realizing we were there.

"What do you want?" His voice was grumpy and raspy.

"We're looking for someone named Samson Hart." Evan told him quickly.

"Not here." The man quickly tried closing the door.

Evan put his arm in the way before the door could fully close. "I think you know what we are looking for, amígo."

The man tried pushing again and Evan pushed harder until the door pushed him back and Evan ran into the house. I followed him and saw that the man had fallen to the floor. I realized Evan was *way* stronger than he looked. My boyfriend grabbed my hand, and we stood in the living room area, or what was left of it. The entire house looked unkempt and abandoned in every way. The stairs had holes in the wood and the furniture had mold on them. There were no pictures or wood for fire and nothing hung up on the walls. The house seemed to be a type of safe house. It looked like the man was here alone.

"What the hell is wrong with you?! This is my house! I didn't tell you to come in!" The man yelled as he struggled to stand up.

"We just need to know if you ever heard of a man named Samson Hart." Evan said calmly as his eyes followed the man whenever he moved.

"Depends on who's asking." The man grumbled.

"Look, just answer the question. Are you Samson?" Evan said, sounding annoyed.

The man sighed. "Yes, I'm Samson. How'd you find me?" He squinted at us.

"I found this." Evan reached into his bag and pulled out the paper he printed the credit card bill onto. "I traced the offshore account number to your phone and found this address."

"Why are you tracking me?" Samson said defensively.

"Do you do any business with my parents?" I blurted out.

"What? Your parents?" Samson looked at me confused and Evan gave me a look that was a warning.

"Yeah, um, we—I traced her parent's credit card bills to see where the payments were being made and the account showed that the activity was being done here. It showed on your phone. We need to know what business you have going on with them." Evan explained.

The man scoffed. "What are you? The police?"

"No. Look, do you know anyone by the name of Ash and Scott Conwell?" Evan's voice sounded strained, like he was talking through his teeth. I could tell that his patience was wearing thin.

Samson looked like he was struggling with whether he should say something. He licked his lips and looked between Evan and I. "Look, I don't know how much I can help you guys, but if there is anything you want to know, I'll do my best to answer." Samson said, looking defeated.

We stared at him for a bit before Evan began speaking. "So, you know her parents?"

"Ash and Scott? Yeah. They came to me a few years ago saying they need some money and an account to wire the cash to."

"You thought nothing of it?" I asked him skeptically.

"Not really. They didn't ask for ridiculous amounts, but they spent a lot at one time. We had an agreement that I would add more money into the account at specific times for specific reasons, but I stopped hearing from them for a while."

"Well, when was the last time you've heard from them?" Evan fished.

"Well, I started helping them in 1989. They started being late for appointments after 1997, and from there, they started becoming like ghosts. Soon, they disappeared completely."

"So, you started helping them after they were bailed out of jail and they slowed down their transactions when they had you, Kassey." Evan put it together.

"You're the one who bailed my parents out?"

"Yeah, they needed money to get out, and they said they would help me if I helped them." He confessed.

"Help them with what?" Evan piped up.

"I became addicted to heroin, and they had some stored in their basement, along with some other things. They said they would give me some supplements if I helped get them money when they needed it." Samson looked at us sheepishly.

"So you made them a deal to get illegal drugs for wiring them money illegally?" Evan sounded disgusted.

"It's not illegal." He said quickly.

"Privately, whatever. The deal is still bad, but it's now void. Now, we need to know if you have an address for us." Evan demanded.

"I-I can't tell you that…" Samson stuttered.

"You said you were going to tell us *everything* we needed to know. Now, if you have an address, we need it." Evan stepped closer to Samson until their chests were touching. Samson was taller than Evan, but Evan was bigger than Samson's skinny build, so they seemed to match each other. He and Samson stared off for a while until I cleared my throat and they both looked at me.

"Please, tell us anything you know. Do you have an address or…something to tell us where they are or could be?" I asked him slowly.

He stared at me for a moment. "I can see what I can do for you."

Evan sighed, but I smiled at Samson. "Thank you, Samson."

He smiled back. "You are welcome. Also, I didn't know they had a daughter. I'm sorry for all the things you must've gone through." He sounded sincere.

I said nothing, and Evan gave the man his phone number before we left. When we got into the car, we both took some time to think about what had just happened.

"So, is that what you wanted?" Evan looked at me.

"Well, it's all I'm going to get, so I kinda have to be ok with it." I said, staring out the windshield.

"No, you don't *have* to be ok with it. We can call it off or—"

"No! I want to see what he finds out. He seemed genuine enough." I cut him off. The thought of calling anything off made my heart drop. We've come this far, and I didn't want to drop anything until we were absolutely finished.

Before Evan drove me back to the house, I asked him to take me to the store. I ran inside and bought three candles. Evan looked at me strangely when I got back into the car, but didn't ask me questions. When he dropped me off, I went into the backyard and found a little spot that looked undisturbed and away from everything else. I dug three little holes and put the three candles into them and lit them. I stared at them and they looked so lonely but peaceful in the afternoon light. I sang a little song for my father and sat outside for a little while. When I determined it was late, I stood up and walked into the house. The next morning, I went to the glass doors and saw that there was ash on the ground and that the candles were gone.

* * * *

It's been weeks since Evan and I had visited Samson. We have heard nothing back, and I believed Evan may have been right. Maybe we couldn't trust him or maybe he knew nothing of use but just wanted to get our hopes up. Evan saw my depression and tried every way he knew to cheer me up, but he wasn't the only one. Everyone seemed to notice my change of mood. Even my teachers laid off of me for a while but still gave me looks from the corners of their eyes. It was driving me crazy. My grades were even lower than average and Hayley brought that to my attention.

"Kassey, what's wrong?" She asked me as I came home from school.

"What do you mean?" I asked as blankly as I could.

She pulled out my grade sheet. "This. You were doing just fine and then I get this. What's going on with you?"

Crap. "Um, it's nothing." I tried avoiding the conversation by going to my room.

She followed. "You can't ignore this."

"What do you want me to tell you?! I suck at school! I hate it! I hate all of this! Why won't you just leave me alone?" I yell at her.

Hayley sighed. "I thought we were getting better."

"With what?"

"You being here. You've had a great relationship with everyone here and everything changed a few weeks ago when you went with your boyfriend to meet his parents. Is that what this is about? Did they not like you? You were gone a long time."

If only she knew. "No, that's not it. They were actually nice."

"So, what is it? Talk to me, Kassey." She pleaded.

I bit my lip and turned my head away. Hayley sighed, frustrated, and left the room. I ran up to my room and threw my bag onto the floor. I closed my eyes and let the tears roll down my cheek. Maybe asking Evan to search for my parents was a bad idea. I couldn't tell anyone but him, and it was tearing me apart to play the waiting game.

When I opened my eyes, I saw Brianna staring at me. I was shocked at first, then confused. What was she doing here?

"Um, hey." I said lamely.

She didn't smile at me, nor did she respond. Was she mad at me?

"Hey." Her voice was quiet. Bri was *never* quiet. Now I was nervous.

"What are you doing here?"

"You've been avoiding me and Emily. You're not talking to anyone and it's getting quite annoying. So, talk." She demanded.

"I-I can't." I stuttered.

Bri scoffed. "What do you mean, you can't? We're friends, right? Aren't we supposed to tell each other everything?"

"Yeah, but—"

"But, what?"

"I just can't. I'm sorry." My voice broke.

Brianna rolled her eyes. "Of course...right. You can't tell me a damn thing, but I tell you everything!"

"You don't tell me *everything*, Brianna." I muttered.

I heard her sigh dramatically. "Well, here's what I have to tell you: You're a liar."

"Wh-what?" Now I was lost.

"You've been keeping too many things from all of us. Your "mom" downstairs was happy to fill me in, and I wonder when you were gonna tell me about you knowing Cameron. You sure spend a lot of energy keeping them out of our conversations." Brianna explained sourly.

I didn't lose my nerve, but my lungs felt like they weren't getting enough air. I really hoped she didn't mean what I think she did. I didn't tell her because of the same reason I didn't tell Evan. I didn't want to be judged. I didn't want to be seen as different or something that didn't belong. That was exactly the reaction I always got. As far as Cameron..that wasn't really my place, nor was it a really big deal. He was a brother, so what? They were exes. That is way too messy to get involved in.

"B-brianna—"

"Don't try to explain your way out. Why didn't you tell me? Emily and I are your best friends. Why didn't you say anything? I can't be trusted or something?" She complained.

"I didn't know how you would react, and I didn't want you to judge me." I whispered.

"So, you automatically assumed how we would feel without actually coming to us?" Brianna summed up.

I slowly nodded. "Yeah…"

"Wow. You really don't know us at all, do you? I don't judge before I know anything. I've never been that way." Brianna said strongly.

"Well, you can't blame me for not saying anything. It's very personal, and it's not something I talk about every single day. Also…you always make situations way more dramatic than they need to be. Hence, right now." I shot back.

I felt a sharp glare come from her. "Damn you. Why are you turning this around on me? You're playing the victim. Always the victim! Why can't you just learn to let people in and to talk to people instead of shutting them out? I am honest with you, but friendship goes both ways, Kassey! As for dramatic, it's not dramatic. I'm upset. So you can quit being a bitch and actually focus on what the real problem is.

Before I could answer, I heard, "Don't waste your breath on this, prick. She's not worth it, Bri." I turned to see Emily coming into the doorway behind Brianna. I scoffed, then sighed. Just when I thought things couldn't get worse…

"So, you're a foster?" Emily asked me.

"Yeah. Apparently." I said sarcastically.

"It's not funny, Kassey. We are supposed to be your friends and—"

"My *real* friends would understand why I had to keep this a secret to myself. They wouldn't try to make me feel bad for not sharing something so personal. Everything that happens to me like this, I may keep to myself. You will not make me feel bad for wanting to keep my personal secrets private." I told them robustly.

They stared at me for a moment without saying anything, Then Brianna scoffed. "That's cute. Try turning it on us, *again*. I bet your boyfriend is more important than us." Brianna shot at me.

"That's different, and I bet you tell all the boys you've been with, everything they want to know."

"Oh, my god. See? That's not fair! We are your friends and you're treating us like we didn't matter enough for something so important!" Brianna yelled.

"*'We are your friends, we are your friends.'* It is my life! Nothing says I have to tell you *every* detail of my life! I'm sorry that you feel less than, but this is my life and my problems. I didn't invite you into my life to have you try to dictate it!" I screamed back.

They both looked at me like I had just spoken a foreign language. Foreign. That was what people thought I was. Foreign. I thought they were different, but they are just like everyone else. They judge you for who you are on the outside rather than the inside. They don't really give you a chance when they see something they don't like. They leave you alone in the dark.

"You know…" Emily started talking and walked around the room. I watched her move around and sit on my bed. It took a lot of my willpower to not yank her up by her weave. "I knew you weren't worth it. Really, did you think anyone would really be your friend when you can't even figure out what you really want? You constantly take without giving back and you don't know, but then things like this happen and you turn into a victim. *Oh, I'm so hurt. Poor me! Poor me, my heart is breaking. My life is falling apart and now I'm gonna lose all of my family, all of my friends, everyone I love. Boo hoo.*" Emily's words dripped with sarcasm and I lost my willpower. I roughly gripped her wrist and yanked her up from my bed, practically throwing her at the wall. She caught herself and pushed herself up so she wouldn't fall to the ground. I received a glare but I barely acknowledged her anymore. I don't talk to two-faced bitches.

"So, what happens now?" Brianna asked. She barely spoke two words since Emily started ripping into me. She was just as fake as Emily.

"Now, I want you to get out of my house." I said solidly.

They both shook their heads and turned to leave. Brianna looked back once they stopped in the doorway. "If more time had gone by, would you have told us in the future?"

"If it felt right, then I would've. Right now, you don't need me telling you something you already know."

"Well, since you think you know everything, check online. Me, being a good friend, I was going to tell you, but...I guess I don't qualify for such a big role." She took Emily's hand and pulled her out of the room.

I heard their footsteps thump down the stairs and the front door slam when they left. I stood there in the middle of my room, trying to understand what had just happened. I had just lost my friends. I hadn't lied to them, had I? I knew I had to tell them sometime, but I didn't expect a blow-out like this. I slowly backed myself up until my legs hit the bottom of my bed and I fell onto it. I stared at the ceiling and didn't move. The house seemed to hold its breath. It was so quiet. There was no movement or sound inside or outside that I could hear.

It was like time had stopped and I was the only one still here.

CHAPTER NINETEEN

It took me a few hours to get over what had happened earlier. I locked myself in my room until I could fully clear my mind and figure out what I was going to do and how I was going to feel about the fight we had. Brianna told me to check online, so I did.

My notifications on social media were overflowing, and I really didn't feel like checking it, but I did. I saw multiple messages from Brianna, Emily, and a few other people wanting friend requests and tagging me.

You have messages from Brianna and Emily.

Brianna: What are you doing?

Brianna: Please answer me, Kassey!

Emily: Did you finish the Spanish homework?

Emily: Please answer Bri so she will stop annoying me.

Brianna: You are in big trouble. WHERE ARE YOU?! Answer me!

You have 3 friend requests and 11 people tagged you in their pictures.

The messages were sent before today, but the last one from Bri, was sent earlier today. Looking at my messages and tags made me wish I checked my phone more often. I looked at my feed to see posts from Brianna with memes that I knew were directed towards me. The thing that made it worse was that she tagged me in everything she posted.

The people who you think you can trust aren't always the ones who are the most faithful.

Those you call friends, aren't they supposed to be ones who you open your mind fully to?

Some things are private in life, yes, but some things should be able to be shared with those you value most.

There were many comments under her posts. Many of them asked her if she was ok. Some people messaged me and asked if our friendship was ok and if the posts were about me. I assumed she had told others what had happened. I shook my head and turned off my phone. My mind was going a mile a minute and social media was making it worse. If she was the one to put her personal business and problems on the internet, she wasn't as mature as she led others to believe.

*   *   *   *

"I'm sorry, Amor." Evan told me during psychology class the next day.

I just shrugged. Fighting with the girls made me feel even more depressed than I was before. I could tell Evan didn't exactly know what to do or say. The only thing on my mind was the fact that I had to see Bri in my next class.

"Look, you don't have to talk to them. They had no right to judge you like that." Evan said protectively.

I gave him a little smile. "Thanks. I wasn't planning on saying anything today, anyway. I mean, what would I say?"

"Whatever feels right. Sometimes, it feels right to not say anything." He suggested.

"Suffer in silence." I muttered, but Evan heard me.

Evan walked me to my math class. He didn't normally do that, only sometimes, but I was glad he did. I would miss him more if he left me alone too early.

"You got this, Amor." He kissed me.

I kissed him back and smiled at him. "Thank you. Um, see you at lunch?"

"Yep. Hot tamales for lunch!" He said excitedly.

I gave him a worried look, and he laughed. When Evan left, I went inside the classroom. I saw Brianna was sitting in her normal seat by the window. I didn't know what else I was expecting. I guess I thought she wouldn't have been here, and it would spared me the humiliation of a conversation that may turn into an argument. When our eyes met, Brianna quickly put her head down. I sighed and went to sit down.

We filled the entire class period with awkward silence between us. We did our work in silence and we read in silence. I caught her a few times looking at me from the corner of her eye when she thought I wasn't looking. I did the same, but I looked through my hair.

We've been friends for months, and now we were like strangers. It was so hard to find words that would start the conversation correctly, so I stayed quiet, like Evan said.

"Why did you sit here?" In the middle of class, Brianna turned to me and spoke in an accusing tone.

"W-what do you mean? I-It's my seat." I was stunned by her sudden words that I stuttered.

"Well, I don't want you anywhere near me, since you aren't truthful. I can't trust you."

What the bloody hell? Wait a minute...Is she calling me a liar? "I don't know what you're talking about, but I'm not moving because I hurt your feelings." I shot at her.

"Well, that's too bad. Things are different now. Move." Brianna toppled over my chair and made me fall to the floor.

Everything stopped in the classroom. The teacher and students looked at me. Some snickered, and some looked genuinely worried, while others just looked tired. I turned towards Bri, but she just smiled at me. I scoffed and stood up, gathered my things, and sat in the closest available seat near me. After staring at us for a moment, Mr. Felix started instruction again.

*　　*　　*　　*

I slammed my locker closed after math class. Oh, my god. I was shaking and suddenly

had a migraine. I have never wanted to scream more than I do now. I wanted to do something

stupid. I wanted to punch something...I wanted Evan. His class was the last to be dismissed

before lunch, so I had to wait. Leaning against my locker and watching crowds of people walk

by me, I saw things differently than I had before. I saw how some people fit with others and how

some didn't. There were labels everyone likes to put on others and mine was entirely different.

"Hey!" I looked up when I heard Evan's voice. I ran up to him and hugged him. Evan

grunted but held me up.

"Dios Mío. What did I do to deserve this?" Evan looked at me, surprised.

"You never left me." I said sadly.

Evan frowned at me and gave me a better hug. I inhaled the scent of him, which

reminded me of the woods we hiked in. He smelled of the outdoors, fresh and full of life.

Untouched and full of bliss. Everything that I needed to have right now.

*   *   *   *

"So, tell me what happened." Evan said as we got seated at his favorite Mexican

restaurant, Casa Mexico. He liked the name because it showed how much the owner really

valued their origin. They loved where they came from and they will shout it to the world. It really struck a cord because I wanted to be proud of my origin, but I didn't really know where that was.

"Um, well, she talked to me after half the class had gone by." I started.

"That's good, right?" Evan asked excitedly.

I shook my head. "Not at all. All she wanted to do was tell me to move because I was too secretive and untrustworthy. She made how she felt pretty clear."

"Oh."

"Then she flipped my chair over with me in it."

Evan choked on his water. I quickly got up and patted his back. "You ok?"

He coughed but gave me a thumbs up as he put the cup down. "I-I'm decent. She—wow. She pushed you over? During class?"

"Yeah." I went back to my seat across from him. "Everyone looked at me like I was crazy, and Brianna just sat there and laughed. I guess I know how she really felt about me in the beginning." My mother would always tell me that people always show their true colors whenever they needed to choose a side.

"What are you talking about, mommy?" I asked my mother during breakfast.

She turned and looked at me. My mother wiped her hands on a towel and took one chair at the table across from me. "Those people you are always crying about? The ones you say always call you names?"

"Yes."

"They are not your friends. No one is really your friend, Kassey. Not even the ones who prove to be loyal. You really can't trust anyone." My mother explained.

"Why not?"

"People show their true colors when they have to choose a side. They deal with you because they have to or because they like you for a little while until they get bored or unamused. Some people are two-faced." My mother had said harshly.

"What is two-faced?" I had stopped eating my breakfast to listen more closely to my mother.

"Someone who is untrustworthy. Someone you really don't know, even if you think you do. They show two different sides of themselves. Those are people you stay away from." My mother had warned me.

"Don't worry mommy. I'll be careful…"

"…Don't worry, Kassey. They aren't worth all the stress. You focus on you and what makes you happy. They'll see what they missed out on." Evan reassured me.

"Thanks." I said, then went back to eating my food.

"No problemo."

My relationship with Brianna and Emily soon became nonexistent. They started hanging out with Robin, who was the worst girl in the school. I didn't mention her before because she was irrelevant. Robin is the girl that people would describe as "The Queen Bee" like the popular group of girls in every high school fantasy. She's annoying, popular, and very updated on everything that happens around her. She doesn't have a group, but she acts like she's in multiple places at once. When I saw Robin and the girls together, at first, I felt left out and abandoned. Then, I realized it doesn't matter that much. It shouldn't have been so easy for them to turn to Robin so quickly. That showed that what my mother had said was true. They didn't really care that much about our friendship. They only tolerated it until they didn't have to anymore.

More time had passed and I still haven't heard anything. By now, I had lost all hope in Samson. If he found anything, we would've heard from him, but I've heard nothing but radio silence. But on another note, I've been with the Johnson's for a year and two months now. I've been counting the days since I've gotten here.

I was lying in my bed when I heard a parade of footsteps coming upstairs. It was a day off from school and I was taking full advantage of that. Waking up early for school had really taken its toll on me. Hearing the footsteps made me skeptical and I sat up just as the door burst opened. Everyone slowly marched into my room in a little crowd of smiling faces.

I looked at them crazily. "What are you guys doing?"

"Happy birthday!" They screamed.

I rolled my eyes. I had actually forgotten it was my birthday. I was 16 today, but I wasn't sure if I was happy about that or not. Hayley came in behind everyone holding a sky blue and crimson cake with a bunch of lit candles on the top. The front of the cake had the words "Happy birthday Kassey" with blue jay birds and lynxes around them.

"I'll admit, I had some help from your boyfriend with the cake. He seems to know you pretty well." Hayley said, sounding embarrassed.

"Well, um, thank you, I guess." I meant it when I told them I would gladly go through my birthday with nothing but a few, "Happy Birthday," shout outs and that's it.

"Well, blow them out before we have a fire." Jason demanded playfully.

I rolled out of bed and thought for a moment before blowing out the candles. They all silently cheered and muttered to each other.

"What did you wish for?" Aliyah asked.

"I can't tell you."

"Why not?" She asked sadly.

"If I told you, then it wouldn't come true." I told her patiently.

"That's silly." Jade chimed in.

"Yeah, it is." I agreed.

I told them all to get out, and they gave me understanding looks and left. I was 16. I didn't know what to think of that. I still hadn't taken my driver's test yet.

My phone rang, and I scrambled to find it before it stopped ringing. "Hello?"

"Happy birthday to you!" Evan sang to me.

"You're all dorks!" I said when he finished the song.

"I guess they gave you the cake, then?"

"And the candles and the song." I added.

"You don't sound happy about any of that." Evan said, sounding cautious.

"Well, they all know that I'm fine with forgetting my birthday."

"Well, I'm not. I promise you, I will make this the birthday of all birthdays!" Evan yelled.

"How do you plan on doing that?" Now was my turn to be cautious.

"Well, I've been planning this for months. That will be for me to know and—"

"I know, 'for me to never figure out.'" I finished for him.

Evan laughed. "Yeah. Be ready in half an hour!"

"But—" He hung up. I growled. Why was he going to make me get dressed this early on my personal weekend?! I knew he was serious, so I went to find a decent outfit.

After taking a shower, I rummaged through my drawers until I found a pair of red-black jeans and a blue t-shirt with the word "Dare" written on the front. I *dare* anyone to say happy birthday to me again today, I thought, then laughed at my thoughts. I put my hair in a ponytail and checked myself in the mirror one last time before going downstairs.

Everyone was talking loudly downstairs, and they all stopped when I came into the kitchen. I didn't acknowledge it when I went to the fridge to get something to drink, but it got weird after a little while.

"Why are you all acting weird?"

"Is there a reason you don't want to celebrate your birthday?" Cameron asked.

"Um, I just don't see the need. It's normally something you do that makes your day happy and when you have someone to celebrate it with." I shrugged at them.

They suddenly looked hurt. "You can celebrate it with us, Kassey." Hayley said as her voice cracked.

"Oh! No...I mean...Look, I've had people forget and I've had short-lived birthdays along with really great ones. I just feel like...acknowledging me getting older will hurt." I tried to explain.

"Is this about you fearing getting older?" Jade asked, chuckling.

"No! I'm not worried about that."

"You want to be with those it really matters to." Jason said matter-of-factly.

I stared at him before muttering, "Yeah, that's exactly why."

"Why didn't you just say that?" Hayley asked me while tilting her head.

"It was hard to explain, and everything I said seemed to be like a dagger to the heart." I said sharply.

"We've kinda gotten used to your harsh words, Kassey."

I looked at Cameron and felt my body get hot. Not from anger, but from embarrassment. I wanted to strike back, but I fought against it. Today was a day that I would not be aggressive. I wanted to have a day that had no drama and no negativity.

"Shut up." I said instead.

"Hayley, can we eat the cake? Pretty please?" Aliyah begged.

"Ask Kassey. It's her cake." Hayley told her daughter, but gave me a look that said, "Just let her have some. It'll make her happy."

Aliyah looked at me hopeful. "Please, sissy?"

My words got stuck in my throat as I looked at the little girl. Did she just call me her sister? "U-um, yeah. You can have some cake." I said, distracted.

"Yay!" Aliyah squealed and waited for Hayley to cut her a piece.

I went off to the open-spaced room to be alone for a while. Aliyah just referred to me as her sister...wow. I knew she and I were close, but we never referred to each other as siblings. Hayley hadn't adopted me yet, and I didn't want to get my hopes up in case she didn't.

"Hey."

I turned to see Jason standing in the doorway, staring at me. I nodded to him but made no motion to move. I was still a thousand miles away.

"So, what's up with you?" Jason walked up to me.

"Did you hear what Aliyah said?" I turned to look at him.

"'Sissy?' yeah. She calls her sisters that. That means she feels close to you. You're her family. That's good." Jason congratulated me.

"Y-yeah. I just wasn't expecting her to say that to me." I gave a little laugh.

"Well, it means you did something right. It also shows that you belong here with us. No one is going to take you away from here." He said seriously.

I bit my lip. I liked being here with the Johnsons, but I always hoped I would be with my parents someday. With Samson being a ghost, that may just be something that may not happen anymore. Maybe Jason was right...or not.

When Evan came, he talked with everyone for a bit, ate some cake, then we both left. He drove us to his house and tried to bring me to his room, but was stopped by his family.

"Feliz cumpleaños, Kassey!" They said when we walked into the living room. I heard Evan groan, but I smiled at all of them.

"Gracias! You didn't have to do this." I didn't know how to say that in Spanish, so I was hoping his siblings would understand.

"We kinda did. Things like this are pretty big in our family and our culture." His sister, Elena, said, smiling.

"Well, thank you." Evan's brother, Nicholás, told his parents what we said.

They gave me a few presents, then Evan yanked me upstairs. When we got to his room, he quickly shut the door and locked it.

"I can't ever get away from them...Dios Mío." He sighed. I realized that this was what he was always going to say from time to time.

"Well, we got away now. So, tell me why you wanted to come up here so bad." I sat on his bed and looked at him.

"Well," He rubbed his hands together like the first time we had met, "I have a few things planned for your big day."

"Uh-oh."

"Don't say that! It's not bad. I promise." He said, allaying. He walked up to me and took my hair out of the ponytail I had put it in. He let my hair fall and put a lock of it behind my ear. "I like it better when you have your hair down. You don't have to be so extra as to change it to impress me."

I avoided looking at him for a moment so he couldn't see my face. "What do you have planned?" I was genuinely interested now so I could steer myself away from the feeling I now had.

"I wrote a song for you." He suddenly sounded embarrassed and his face got a little red.

I was enjoying this side of Evan. "You wrote me a song?"

"Y-yeah. Only if you want to hear it…"

"Damn straight, I want to hear it!" That was my favorite thing to say. I kinda laid off of it for a while, but I still enjoyed the words, "Damn straight."

Evan grabbed his guitar and went to his desk to grab some papers that were stacked in a neat pile. He sat on his bed and I moved myself so I could see his face and hands better. While Evan got himself together, I was fascinated with the way he moved his fingers over the strings when he tried to familiarize himself with the notes. I couldn't play an instrument, but those who could always amazed me.

Evan started playing the notes, and they sounded beautiful to me. He played each cord carefully, but also expertly. The song sounded more like a poem than a song, but I loved it just the same because it came from him.

"The day we first met was the day my life started,

You hid yourself and cast a glamor.

You were the one who was so brokenhearted,

Mí amor, Mí amor..."

Evan didn't look at me as he played, but I could tell he was waiting for a reaction. I loved the way he sang and kept up with the notes he played. Before, he told me he couldn't sing, but he was wrong. Coming from someone who was listening to him, he had a beautiful voice.

"...I have never been happier,

I have never felt more alive.

You are my girl, you're my great divine…"

Evan looked at me and smiled. I had closed my eyes during the song as I listened to what he was saying. I didn't know he felt this way when he first saw me. He appeared to be a cool but sometimes awkward boy I met in psychology class. Evan wasn't one to show or explain out loud how he was feeling. I guess music was a way he enjoyed trying to explain himself.

"...I see you now! I hear your voice!

You never have to hide from me!

You'll never have to make a choice,

We will finally be free!

The day we first met was the day my life started,

You hid yourself and cast a glamor.

You were the one who was so brokenhearted,

Mí amor, Mí amor."

I sang with him this time since I knew the lyrics he was going to sing. I could tell it threw him off, but his notes didn't falter. It only seemed to encourage him to sing louder, and me as well. I was having fun and then I realized he had never heard me sing.

"...Tu, Mí amor,

Estoy contenta contigo.

You will never have tristeza,

There will never be time to be blue.

You are my flower,

Tu es mi familia.

You help me see my happiness,

You are my honey, mí pamelia.

The day we first met was the day my life started,

You hid yourself and cast a glamor.

You were the one who was so brokenhearted,

Mí amor, Mí amor."

When Evan ended his song, he gently put his guitar down and looked at me. I could still hear him singing and was sad the song ended. I opened my eyes after closing them too many times and tried to figure out what to say.

"So?" He waited.

"I loved it!" I jumped on him and he gave me a half hug as he tried to avoid getting his instrument damaged.

"Wow, um, thanks." He sounded embarrassed.

"Stop being so modest. You said you couldn't sing." I squinted my eyes at him.

"I can't."

"Yes, you can. Take it from someone who just heard you." I encouraged him.

"You're my girlfriend. You have to be nice." He shook his head.

"I can be biased, but I'm serious. I like how you sing." I smiled at him.

He turned his head away for a moment before smiling back. "I like your singing, too. I've never heard you sing before."

"Well, I don't sing that much anymore." I said sadly.

"You should. It sounds good." He gently touched my cheek before standing to put everything away.

"So, what's next on your agenda?" I watched him as he cleaned up.

"Hm...I was thinking I would take you to Tybee again like we did before. If you wanted."

"The beach?!" I got excited.

I heard him chuckle. "Yes, Amor. I'll take that as a 'I want to go.'"

"I want to go! I want to go! I want to go! I want to go!" I squealed and clapped.

"Oh, my god, calm down! You're going to make someone come in here!" He shushed me.

"That's the first time you said 'Oh, my god' in English." I told him, giggling, but I stopped jumping and clapping.

Evan drove us to the island, and we went swimming again. It was hotter out today so the water was exceptionally cold and felt amazing! I was actually enjoying my birthday. I just wished my friends were here to celebrate with us.

"What's wrong?" Evan asked me as we sat down on the towel he had brought.

"I know this is irrelevant, but I wish the girls were here." I said, while facing the waves.

"It's not irrelevant. I understand why, but they messed things up with you, not the other way around. Also, they replaced you the next day. They weren't your real friends, Kassey." Evan wrapped his arm around me.

I leaned on his shoulder. "I know. I'm glad I have you."

"I'm going nowhere. I'll always be here for you. I promise." Evan played with my hair and rubbed my scalp for a little while until we both became hungry. We toured the boardwalk until we found some decent food. He sat us down on a bench and we talked for a while. I got to tell him more about how I felt about his song.

"So you *really* liked it?" He asked me again.

"Yes! Do you think I'm lying to you?" I asked him as I took a bite of my sandwich.

"No, I just...wanted to be sure." He shrugged.

I shook my head. "I'll be back." I stood up and went to find a bathroom.

CHAPTER TWENTY

While washing my hands, I reached for the soap, and it was empty. I sighed and reached for the towels, but they weren't there either. Who stocks these bathrooms?! I air dried them and went to leave when I heard someone call my name from behind me.

"Hello?" I angled my head towards the stalls.

It was a small bathroom. There were three stalls, two sinks, and a door. If anyone wanted to hide, they would have to hide in a stall.

"If someone's there, you better come out! It's not funny!" I yelled.

I still heard the whisper of my name and I finally pushed past my pride to walk up to the stalls. I walked by each of them, swung them open, and found them all empty.

What? Maybe I was losing my mind. I shook my head and mentally kicked myself for yelling at nothing. I tried to get myself together, then ran right into someone when I turned around.

"Oh, sorry." I apologized, then froze when I saw his face.

He smiled down at me. "Hey there."

"K-Khalil—w-what…" I stammered.

"Why are you so flustered?" He followed me as I kept backing away from him.

"Why are you in the girls' bathroom?" I had so many questions I could've asked and my brain picked the stupidest one. I silently chastised myself.

Khalil chuckled. I knew he could see how wound up I was. "I missed you, Kase. I wanted to talk before. I know I may have come off a little strong, but I promise everything will be fine this time. Just let me explain."

"Get out. Leave me alone. I don't want to see you and I want nothing to do with you!" I pushed him, but he didn't really move. He was stronger than I was. That was why I had always hated him. He had so much power over me because he made me feel smaller than he was. Khalil grabbed my arms and pushed me against the bathroom stall. I tried pulling away from him, but he kept pushing me back each time I tried. He slid his hands down my arms until he reached my wrists, and increased the pressure he had on them until it felt like my circulation was being cut off. I went to scream, and he clamped his hand over my mouth.

"Don't scream." He whispered. His hand slowly moved, and he put his hands on my cheeks. "You don't have to be afraid. I would never hurt you."

"You took advantage of me! I trusted you!" I said, wailing.

"That's all in the past. We can start over. I was young, and you were, too. We didn't know any better." He claimed.

"You were supposed to protect me. You were supposed to care for me *as a brother!* I had no feelings for you romantically! You forced that onto me. I didn't want you like you wanted me!" I yelled at him.

I heard knocking on the door, followed by a woman's voice. I had turned the knob to show the bathroom was occupied and now immediately regretted it. Wait...I locked the door. How did he…

"How did you even get in?" Khalil had let me go and my eyes followed him as he paced around the bathroom.

"It doesn't matter. I'm here now." He walked back towards me at a fast pace and I quickly tried to move away from him again. Khalil grabbed my shoulders and pulled me towards him like he did the last time. I glared at him with as much venom as I could, but he didn't seem to care. He angled his head and started kissing my neck. My arms and legs were immobilized, and it felt like there was ice in my veins. Everything hurt and my surroundings suddenly weren't as clear as they should've been.

"Please leave me alo—" I felt his lips on mine and my mind screamed for me to back away. When I tried, his hold on me became stronger until my whole body felt like it was on fire and totally immobilized. He deepened the kiss, and I felt totally grossed out. When the muscles in my legs unfroze, I kneeled him in his stomach. Khalil doubled over and let go of me. I ran toward the door and tried to work to get it open, but my fingers were shaking so hard that I couldn't really bend them to grab the knob. I finally wrenched the door open when I felt something grab my hair. I fell back and was thrown until I hit the bathroom wall. I grunted as my head hit the hard corner and everything was thrown out of focus.

Everything hurt. My legs, arms, neck, and head. I slowly raised my hand to touch the back of my head and felt something warm run down my scalp and the back of my neck to my back. I slowly raised my head to look at him as he walked up to me. Khalil kneeled down and grabbed my chin to pull my head up and look at him.

"Hmm...you are one hardheaded girl."

My head pounded, and everything remained out of focus. I tried to think of where my phone was and I silently cursed myself when I realized it was in the car. I was wearing a bathing suit that Evan had bought for me to wear today, and it had no pockets. Khalil looked me over and a smile slowly formed itself on his face. He gave me a sneer-like look, then let me go. I felt like I couldn't breathe. My chest felt hot, like it was on fire, and I couldn't move my body no matter what I did. I knew something was broken.

"If you ever cared about me, it shouldn't be so easy for you to hurt me." I choked.

"Oh, now you talk about caring for each other. You fought me every step of the way. Have you finally realized I was right?" Khalil looked at me skeptically.

"I will *never* have feelings for you and I will never want to go back to you, Amelia, or anyone else in that home. I just want you to leave me alone." Khalil's figure flashed in front of me in a blur and I felt pressure on my throat. I gagged and clawed at his arm. He looked at me with so much hatred and sadness that I soon grew scared. Was he trying to kill me? Was everything he talked about before true? He never released the pressure, and my throat felt like it was closing up and my windpipe was being crushed.

"K-Khalil!" I uttered.

"You little ungrateful—"

"Hey! What are you doing?!" I heard a familiar voice and sent a little silent thank you prayer to anyone who would listen. I felt the pressure decrease, then disappear. I couldn't really see who had helped me, but I saw two figures go at it for a while before it became too hard to focus on anything.

"Kassey? Kassey!" The blur came back into my view, but I could barely keep my eyes open enough to put together a face. I didn't know how delirious I was, but I felt myself being lifted into the air and moved away from where I was. I had been fighting to stay awake, but my body was now screaming in pain and exhaustion.

"Kassey, stay awake. Please stay awake…" The voice sounded so far away. I wanted to stay with them, but my body wasn't letting me. My eyelids felt like they were getting heavier by the minute and my body was feeling colder by the second. I didn't know what was going on, but I felt my strength leave me until there was nothing left but darkness.

CHAPTER TWENTY-ONE

I opened my eyes to a brightly lit room. I didn't know where I was, but I knew I wasn't in my room. I felt stiff and very heavy. I slowly turned my head from side to side to try and gather my surroundings. As everything became more clear, I realized I was in the hospital. How did I get here? What happened? I felt something poke me and saw there was a needle in my arm. I despised needles. I went to pull it out, but felt a hand grab mine.

"Don't do that." A familiar voice said. It took me a minute to figure out who it was, and when I did, I was overcome with overwhelming happiness.

"Evan! Oh, Evan!"

"Calm down, Amor! Please. You'll hurt yourself." He said, sounding worried.

"I don't care. I need to tell you—"

"You got attacked. I know. I was the one who found you." He sounded angry.

"I'm sorry."

"Who was the guy who hurt you? Do you remember what happened?" Evan questioned.

"He was a foster brother I had a few years ago. I didn't like the home or the children. I hated him the most." Talking about Khalil was like having a panic attack repeatedly. You never wanted to relive it.

"He abused you?" Evan guessed.

"He took advantage of me." I whispered. Since telling my siblings, it was still hard to say it out loud, but it wasn't as impossible as it was before.

I heard Evan growl. "And he thought he could still have something with you?! That's illegal!"

"I don't think it's illegal...per se..."

"You're defending him?" He still sounded mad, but I also heard hurt in his voice.

"No! Never! I would never defend him! I'm just saying… I don't know what he was thinking about trying to...have anything to do with me that way." I felt nauseated just talking about this.

"Are you ok? You look sick." He went back to being worried.

"No, I'm not. Can we...can we talk about something else? Please?" I said weakly.

Evan nodded. "I called your family and they've been waiting for you to wake up."

"How long have I been asleep?" I just realized that I didn't know what day or month it was.

"You've been asleep for two weeks. Today's March 5. Everyone's worried. We even thought you wouldn't wake up. You were pretty banged up. Even the guys came to check up on you." Evan explained.

"W-weeks?" March? I stared at him, dumbfounded. Was I really hurt that badly?

There were so many people that came into the room when the doctor came to check up on me. They all looked at me with two expressions: pity and worry.

"What are the injuries?" Hayley asked him.

"Well, she has a mild concussion and skeletal bruising, which needed stitches for cuts. There was also some internal bleeding, as well as fractions on her ribs, arms, and legs that we also had to tend to." The doctor explained.

Everyone was quiet for a moment. "Thank you." Evan finally said.

The doctor left, and the room was still quiet. No one knew the right words to say or how to make things seem better. It seemed like, if anyone talked, it would suck out the air in the already-hard-to-breathe room.

"How are you feeling?" Jason asked me.

"Like I got run over multiple times with a truck." I groaned.

"You'll feel better. You did last time." Cameron commented.

"Shut up, Cam!" Jason hissed.

"It's fine. He's right. No hospital is going to keep me down, right?" I reassured them. Some of them smiled, but others still looked worried. "Guys, really. I'm fine."

"Why does he keep attacking you?" Jade asked.

"He's psychotic. That's why." Jason said angrily.

"Evan…" I looked at him, then at his friends.

He blinked at me. "Oh! Um, these are my guys: Aiden, Oliver, and Quinn. They've been wanting to meet you for a while." Evan introduced them.

"Nice to meet you, Kassey." Oliver said.

"Evan never shuts up about you." Aiden complained.

I giggled, then started coughing, which changed to groaning as my chest hurt. Hayley, Jason, and Evan came forward to help me.

Hayley gave me some water. "Are you ok?"

"I forgot not to move…or breathe." I gave her a small smile, but it felt forced.

"You'll be fine, Kassey." Aliyah chimed in. She came beside my bed and gave me one of her cheerful smiles and a small pat on my hand.

I smiled at her. "Thanks, love."

They had me stay overnight for one more observation to see how critical my condition was. Evan stayed with me when the doctor told everyone to go back home. Hayley, Jason, and the girls didn't want to leave, but I told them I would be fine if Evan stayed.

When the room cleared out, Evan spoke in a serious voice. "Everyone's gone. You can be honest now."

"What do you mean?"

"How are you *really* feeling? I'm the only one here, so you don't have to put on a show." He tilted his head at me.

I opened my mouth, but no sound came out. He waited, and I sighed. "Ok, I feel like I went to hell and back twice. That was a sucky way to end my birthday."

"I'm sorry. If I had known…"

"You couldn't have known. I didn't, either, but I'll be fine. I think they'll let me out tomorrow." I said hopefully.

Evan's phone rang, and he walked out to answer it. I leaned back onto the pillow and looked at the ceiling. It reminded me of the cement block walls in jail. My heart jumped when that word entered my mind and repeated itself in my head. I was reminded of what Samson said about my parents and what Evan had searched for. I didn't know where they were, but my mind kept going toward the possibility that they were locked up. The thought made me fidgety. I shook my head, as if to shake out the thoughts, and closed my eyes.

"You're not going to think of this, Kassey. Just let it go. Stop stressing yourself out." I whispered to myself. I closed my eyes and wished for sleep to come and take me away from the dark thoughts.

*   *   *   *

The hospital released me the following week, but told me to lie low for a while.

"Don't worry. We'll take good care of her." Hayley assured them.

Hayley brought me back to the house by noon. She and the kids had some food fixed for me in the kitchen and they already made my bed. Hayley helped me sit down at the table and watched me closely as I ate my food.

"Is it alright? Do you like it?" Hayley suddenly asked.

"It's fine, Hayley." I told her as I took a bite of my sandwich.

"I know you don't eat the majority of the things we eat, and I don't know any…"

"Vegan foods?" I finished for her.

She chuckled. "Yeah, I just wanted you to feel comfortable."

"Well, I'm good. You did good, thanks." I wiped my hands on a napkin she gave me. "I'm going to take a shower."

"Ok, please be careful, Kassey." She said as I walked up the stairs.

"Will do, captain." I saluted the air and went up to my room.

My room was so neat that it was scary. I mean, I'm not a messy person. My room is what they call "messy clean." I knew where everything was and my room wasn't so dirty that it would be alarming. Right now, my room looked like elves cleaned it.

I shook my head and slowly got to the floor to look for my box, which was still in the same spot where I left it. I smiled and reached for it, and grimaced when my body rejected the movement. I pulled off the lid and took out some pictures. I stared at faded backgrounds and big smiles. I read each back for notes and only one actually had writing. It was a picture of when I was born and my parents were holding me at their house. The back read: Our little girl is born.

She will be showered with love, promises, and opportunities. We love you, our Kassey. Grow to be the woman we will be proud to call our daughter. February 20, 1997.

I put all my photos back in the box and put the box back under my bed. I missed them more each time I looked at a photo or read one of their notes. *Stop thinking about them, Kassey. Remember, you are focusing on things that won't stress you out. If you were going to find them, Samson would've told you something by now. It's been months. Let it go and focus on yourself and your life.*

Right. I needed to stop obsessing over every brief minute that my phone would go off or the doorbell would ring with some new piece of information. I needed to focus on my life and everything that goes with that. I finally got myself to take a shower and get dressed in clean clothes. I've been wearing the same clothes the hospital gave me. They had become attached to my skin and smelled of blood, sweat, and medicine. I was trying to find a shirt when I heard a knock on the door.

"Hey, um, Hayley wants you to—oh! Sorry!" Cameron had come into my room but was quickly backing out when I turned to look at him.

"It's fine, Cam." I had just found a shirt and quickly put it on so he wouldn't feel embarrassed anymore. "You can come back in."

He peeked his head into the room and slowly came back in. I saw his cheeks blush as he looked at me, then looked away. I felt a smile slowly spread across my face. I never really saw Cameron embarrassed, so this was an important moment.

"What did Hayley need?" I prompted him.

"Um..she needs you to come downstairs." He stammered through his sentence.

"Thanks. I'll be down there soon." I told him. Cameron nodded and quickly exited the room. I giggled once he was gone. I had never seen Cameron that way. He was visually embarrassed and he couldn't hide it any better than I could hide my laughter.

When I came downstairs, everyone was standing beside the staircase. I slowed my pace as I approached them. What was going on?

"We were going to do this on your birthday, but with everything that happened, we weren't able to." Hayley started.

"So, what are you doing? What is all this?" I asked them. Everyone had little wrapped up boxes in their hands.

"They were for your birthday!" Aliyah said excitedly.

"We can still give them to you now. If you want them." Jade said, shrugging.

"Lets see what you guys got." I winked at them and followed them to the living room.

I sat down on the big couch with Aliyah and Jason, while Hayley and Jade sat on the smaller couch, and Cameron sat on the loveseat. Aliyah screamed that she would give her present first, so everyone allowed her to start. When I opened it, I saw a little notebook that had, "Mine belongs to me," written on it. When I went to open the book, it already had a few pages used.

"Aliyah, is this yours?"

She nodded. "Hayley gave it to me. I wanted you to have it. I know you were running out of pages in your book, so I wanted to give you mine!" Aliyah giggled and looked at me like she had the best idea in the universe.

"I can't take this from you, Aliyah. It's not fair." I tried giving it back to her, but she just shook her head and waved her hands at me.

"I *want* you to have it, Kassey. We are sisters now! I get to share my things with you!" She said happily.

I finally gave in and thanked her for the gift. I moved onto Cameron's gifts, which were R&B concert tickets that didn't have an expiration date and a signed basketball. I looked at him with a face of surprise.

"Evan told me about how you like basketball, so I found one that was signed by Shannon Bogues. Evan said you liked him...and the rap tickets." Cameron explained when he saw my expression.

"I like him because I like basketball and we have the same birthday." I told him. I stared at the basketball in awe. "You really didn't have to do this, Cameron."

"I had no need for it. Plus, I knew you would like it, and it would make up for all the times I was terrible to you." Cameron shrugged nonchalantly, but I saw a small smile on his face.

"Mine next." Jason gave me his present. It was an empty photo book. "I wanted to give you something that would be memorable. You can choose to do whatever you want with it."

Jade's present was a sketchbook and an mp3 player. It didn't have any songs programmed on it. I thanked her and went to Hayley's present, which was a folder of pictures of the kids, my foster parents from past years, and my own parents. I looked at her sharply. How did she get these?

"Where did you get these of my parents?"

"Well, the pictures of us are pictures I have all over the house. The ones of your parents—I asked some of your guardians from past years to see if they had any I could have and give to you. I wanted something to give to you that would be memorable, too." Hayley explained.

"We collaborated." Jason added.

"Well, um, thank you. I really like them. You really didn't have to do this." I tried to wrap up each present and put them back neatly in their boxes.

"You are our sister. We kinda have to. Plus, it was a good way to make up for the crazy birthday." Jade said.

"Jade, not cool." Jason said sharply.

"No, she's right. I don't have the best fortune with good days." I took all my presents and went to put them in my room. I heard Jason quietly chastising Jade, and I shook my head. Jason always had my back, whether or not I wanted him to. When I heard someone call my name from downstairs, I came back down and saw that everyone was crowded by the door.

"What's going on?"

When I rounded near the end of the stairs, I saw that there were two police officers in the doorway.

CHAPTER TWENTY-TWO

I stood frozen on the stairwell. I hated the police with every part of me. What were the police doing here? What did I do now? Who called the cops?

"Kassey, please come down." Hayley's voice sounded strained.

I made my legs work to descend the stairs. I saw that Aliyah was hiding behind Hayley, and she had her arm wrapped around her. Cameron, Jade, and Jason were in the kitchen, but I could feel their intensity from where I was. I moved closer to Hayley as I moved away from the stairwell. Hayley subconsciously grabbed my hand, and I didn't move away. I looked at the two men. One had a hat on, with black hair cropped a little too short and graying a little. He looked to be about in his late-thirties. The other cop looked younger, maybe mid-twenties. He had a short, neatly trimmed beard and long hair that created a curtain over his right eye.

"What can we do for you, officers?" Hayley asked quietly.

"Which one of you is Kassey Conwell?" The older one asked. His voice was deep, like a baritone.

"Why? Who's asking?" Cameron challenged.

I heard Jade shush him. I looked at the two men and wanted to speak up, but Hayley squeezed my hand as a notion to stand still. I was becoming really nervous. My mind suddenly went to Evan. Did the police go to his house, too? What did they want?

"Which one of you is Kassey?" The officer's voice sounded annoyed. I looked at his shirt and saw that his tag read "Wolf."

"I am." My voice sounded stronger than I felt, and I was so glad for that. I could feel Hayley stiffen and I could feel everyone staring holes into my back, but I didn't break my cool posture.

"We need you to come with us." The younger one said. He seemed to be the more calm and cheerful one.

"Where is she going?" Hayley's voice sounded stronger.

"She needs to come with us to the station. We need her to answer some questions for us." Wolf stated.

"Why can't she answer them here?" Jason asked quickly.

"Guys, it's ok. I'll go." I didn't want to argue with the cops. I never have. If they just wanted some answers to questions, then I could do that.

"Just give us a minute, please." I didn't see Hayley's face, but I could imagine her giving them a death stare.

"Not too long, ma'am." The cheerful one said with a smile. I tried reading his nametag, but he walked out before I could. I'm guessing he was the one to smooth things over and make people feel comfortable being around a cop. I made a quick decision in my head that I liked him more than I liked "Wolf."

"You don't need to go. Don't let them bully you into going with them, Kassey."

Everyone came from where they were and gathered around Hayley and I. Cameron started immediately on dismissing the idea of me leaving with two cops.

"I don't like cops anymore than you do. They just want to ask me a few things. I'll do that and be right back. I know I didn't really do anything." I think I was saying this to reassure myself more than I was trying to reassure them.

"Don't answer questions you don't want to. Do you need a lawyer?" Hayley asked quickly.

"No, Hayley. I'll be fine." I gave her the most convincing look I could give her and went outside to the cop car that was waiting by the sidewalk. When I got inside, they waited for me to buckle in before they drove off.

*   *   *   *

The ride was quiet, but I couldn't follow the pol—men out of the car. I looked at the department and I froze up again. What did they really want from me? Did I do something wrong? The friendly cop opened the door and looked at me with a face of concern and confusion.

"I think the point of a car is to get in and get out." He joked.

"I can't. Do I really need to be here?" I didn't look at him. I didn't want him to read my face.

"You don't have to be nervous. Trust me." I risked it and turned my head towards him. When I did, I saw his nametag read "Portman". Whenever a cop says, "Trust me," it's in your best interest to do the *exact* opposite. I sucked it up and marched my way through the police department. They sat me down in a chair in the interrogation room and left me alone for a while. I got to thinking to myself for a bit and I wanted to call Evan, but they took my phone before I came into the room.

A few minutes later, a guy came in and sat in the chair across from me. He was a bald man with auburn eyes. He wore a black suit, black suit pants, and dress shoes. The way he sat down was the way a boss would sit down in his office. He seemed to be very confident. He leaned forward and clasped his hands together as he sized me up and down. I didn't move. Something about this man made me uneasy. I didn't like him and he seemed to be the type to mix up your words.

"So, you are Kassey, right?" He started. His voice was raspy.

"Who's asking?" I kept my face as blank as I could.

"My apologies. My name is detective Abott. We've been trying to track you for a while."

"Why? What do you want from me? What could I possibly give to you that would be beneficial?" I crossed my arms.

"What do you know about your parents?" The detective ignored my questions.

"M-my parents?" It was becoming harder to hide my feelings from the detective. "What does this have to do with my parents?"

"We've been tracking your parents for years now, especially when we found you. They left you behind and we didn't really know anything about you. I'm hoping you could fill in the blanks for us." He explained. Abott never took his eyes away from my face.

"I can try."

I watched as Mr. Abott pulled out a notebook and a pen. He looked up at me when he was ready. "Alright. How old are you?"

"16." I kept my answer short. My dad always said, when being questioned by a police officer or a detective, don't give too many details. Just a straightforward answer.

"When was the last time you saw your parents?"

"I don't really know...maybe when I was four." My brain worked slowly for this question. I really didn't remember exactly when I last saw them. I just knew that I was in another place with other people when I was four. I never paid attention to anything else.

"Do you know anything else about your parents? Anything important?" He pushed.

"I don't really know anything. They left when I was really young and they were good to me." That was a half lie, and I knew it. I knew a little more than what I was saying, but my parents were good people. They were good to me and that was all that mattered to me.

"What do you remember from the night that they left?"

"I don't really remember anything."

"Is there anything else you can tell—"

"What do you know about me?" I shot at him.

I can see that my question threw him off a little, but he wasn't entirely taken aback. "Excuse me?"

"What do you know about me that you consider important?" I asked him again.

He shook his head. "Some guys in our department found you in your parent's home when you were…" He checked his folder that he brought in, "...You were indeed four when the police found you. They rushed you to the hospital, you received treatment, and then were sent into the foster care system." He explained.

Exactly what Evan found. "Why am I here, detective?"

Mr. Abott chuckled. "You're a hard kid. We wanted to ask you some questions and then show you something. Now that this is done, will you mind following me?" He got up and headed towards the door. He stopped at the door and waited till I got up and followed him.

The detective had me sit in a place that looked like a school cafe. There were many inmates meeting with their families, friends, and spouses. I sat at an empty table, wondering why I was here. Who was I waiting for? Why couldn't I wait in an office or something? I glanced over and saw a glare of an orange jumpsuit not too far from where I was. I leaned forward and saw a familiar face, Samson, as they hauled him to a cell behind the gate. The face he gave me when our eyes met was one to make you want to lower your head. Well, that explains the radio silence.

"Kassey!"

I turned when I heard someone yell my name, well scream really. Evan was running like the devil was behind him. I wasn't able to turn all the way around before he collapsed onto me. He knocked the wind out of me and I couldn't really hold him up, but I was glad he was here.

"E-Evan..."

"Dios mío, I'm so glad you are ok!"

"Y-yeah. I-I can't b-breathe." I gasped.

"Oh, sorry." He quickly let me go and looked at me with a sheepish smile. "I think I got a little too happy."

"It's ok. I'm glad you're here."

"Jason called me and told me you were here. I just thought that you may have done something or…" He trailed off.

"You thought this was my fault?" I pretended to be offended.

"Oh! No! I just—"

"I'm joking, Evan. Relax." I giggled.

"Oh. That wasn't funny. How are you so calm?" He wiped his forehead.

"Trust me, I'm not as calm as I look. I'm screaming inside. I just learned that it's not good to show too much emotion in front of cops, especially in the police station." I restated what my parents told me.

Evan nodded. "True. Why are you sitting here?" He sat down in the space next to me.

"I don't know. They just told me to wait here."

"Weird. I don't trust cops." Evan crossed his arms.

"Me neither." I looked up when I heard the gate open and saw two police officers shuffling two inmates, a man and a woman, into the room. The prisoners looked angry and tired. I thought nothing of it until they came up to our table. I felt Evan reach for my hand when they kept coming closer. Who were these people and why were they coming towards us? Is this the reason I was sitting here?

The officers forced the inmates onto the bench and went back toward the gates that separated the cells from the cafe. Me, Evan, and the prisoners stared at each other for a while in awkward silence.

"Um, hey." Evan said, trying to fill the silence.

The two prisoners looked at each other, then went back to studying us. I cleared my throat, and the woman looked at me.

"Do you know why we are here?" I asked them slowly.

"No, we don't." The man's tone was sharp, but I didn't flinch. The woman wouldn't stop looking at me, and I was starting to feel uncomfortable.

"Scott...look at her." The woman whispered.

Scott? Why did that name sound familiar? I wrecked my brain trying to figure it out.

We stared at him for a bit before Evan began speaking. "So, you know her parents?"

"Ash and Scott? Yeah. They came to me a few years ago saying they need some money and an account to wire the cash to."

Scott...Scott was the name Samson gave us when we asked about my parents. It was a long shot. I mean, there are many people with the same name. It could just be a coincidence.

"Scott?" Evan looked at me. I think he had the same thought I had.

"Yeah, that's my name. Who are you?" The man asked boredly.

"I'm Evan and this is my girlfriend, Kassey. "

"Kassey? Kassey, is that you?" The woman asked, sounding like she found the world's lost treasure. I looked at her like she had lost her mind.

"Yeah...?"

"I'm Ash and this is Scott. I was hoping we could see you someday."

"Ash and Scott. You're the ones that got arrested on December 1, 2000?" Evan asked them carefully.

"Who are you? A lawyer?" Scott leaned forward and tried to stare Evan down.

"We had a daughter named Kassey. We haven't seen her in a long time. You look just like her." Ash stared at me as she talked. As I looked at her, her features looked familiar. She looked like my mother.

"How old was she when you left?" I asked. I didn't want to get my hopes up just yet.

"She was four. She had on her cute little basketball shorts and red shirt. She would always carry around a little basketball her father gave her or the doll that I gave her." Ash explained.

"It was a crimson shirt, not red." I muttered absentmindedly. I hated it when there was a specific color and people only said the main one. Like red with crimson or green with emerald.

The woman's eyes lit up when I responded to what she said. I didn't think she heard me. What she said about what I wore that night was correct. Looking at these people in front of me, and their familiar features, they looked exactly like my parents.

"Mom?" I whispered slowly.

In the corner of my eye, I saw Evan look at me, then turn back to face my dad.

The table was quiet again. No one knew what else to say. I just wanted to stare at them and compare the features in front of me with the ones I had in my memory. The Ash and Scott I saw now looked older and more troubled, but they still looked like my parents.

"You grew so much." Ash raised her hand but stopped as she remembered where she was. "I'm so sorry we had to leave you. I hope you understand why."

"You're criminals and you didn't want to make it look like a four-year-old child was helping you deal drugs?" I asked sarcastically.

Ash flinched, but Scott just turned his attention to me. "Watch your mouth."

"I think you better watch how *you* speak to her." Evan growled.

"Will everyone shut up for a minute?" I gave each of them a look and saw one man turn and stare at us with a sharp look. When he saw me looking at him, he nodded his head and turned away. I considered that as a warning.

"Look, we all found each other. Great. Why did you leave me behind like that? The police found me and took me to a hospital! They didn't know what was wrong with me! How could you leave a child you claim to love so much?" I could hear the raw emotion in my voice, but I was determined to get some answers from them. All these years of being without them, they at least owed an explanation.

"We never wanted to leave you. Your father said it would be too dangerous for a four-year-old child to be with us. He was right. The only logical thing to do was to leave you here and have you taken care of by a loving family." Ash explained.

"Dios Mío. That's the best you could come up with?" Evan asked, unconvinced.

"What do you mean? I'm telling the truth! You can choose not to believe me, but I mean what I say. I wanted you to have a family to take care of you when we couldn't." Ash looked at me pleadingly.

"If you wanted me to feel loved, then you should've stayed. You should've stopped what you were doing so you wouldn't have a reason to leave in the first place! I am your daughter and I should've been your priority! You cared more about your *job* than your child!" I yelled at them.

Ash looked like she was close to tears. Scott looked at me like I was the worst person in the world. I've always had a closer relationship with my mother, but my father was never this cold. However long he had been here, he changed from the man he was twelve years ago.

"Do you remember the day that you had that terrible cold and couldn't get out of bed? Do you remember what I said to you?" Ash asked as she deflected the conversation.

I sighed. "Yeah, I do."

"Mommy...my head hurts…" I coughed.

I couldn't see as clearly, but I saw my mom sit on the edge of my bed and place her hand on my forehead.

"You're sick, honey. You'll be alright. I promise." She smiled at me.

"No, I'm going to die." I moaned.

Her face turned to horror. "No! Never say that. It's just a cold, Kassey. Nothing is going to happen to you. I will let nothing happen to you. I promise you that."

"Mommy, will you promise to stay with me?" I was feeling tired, but I was terrified of the thought of my mother leaving me alone.

"I will. I'll stay with you. Don't worry about anything. I will take care of you." My mother kissed my cheek and gave me a smile that I couldn't help returning.

"I meant what I said, and you got better, didn't you?" Her voice cut into my retrine.

"Yeah, I did."

"How can you explain being gone for so long? Why didn't you try reaching out to her or letting her know you were ok?" Evan asked them. He sounded like he wasn't buying anything they were saying.

"We wanted to, but it would compromise things for us if we did." My father spoke up.

"For you? What about me? I was worried sick all my life about you two! I didn't know where you were or if you were still alive. I've been in so many homes, good and bad. You've missed so much of my life that you do not know who I am." I accused them. I felt tears prickle the back of my eyes, but I forced them to stay there. I refused to cry in front of them.

"It wasn't like that. We didn't mean to worry you and...I'm sorry we missed so much of your life. I'm sorry we missed your birthday." Ash quickly reached over to grab my arm and I hissed as pain spread through my arm. Evan's head twisted toward me. I yanked my arm back and saw hurt and confusion spread through my parent's faces.

"You ok?" Evan whispered to me.

"I'm ok." I whispered back. My arm felt like electrical currents were running through my veins. I hadn't exactly gotten better from being in the hospital, but I thought I was better than I felt now. My mother had caught me off guard by reaching for me. It brought back memories I didn't know were still there.

"NO!" I screamed as I ran to my room. I heard footsteps running after me, but I didn't stop until I closed the door. I ran to my bed and crawled under it. I could hear my breath coming in fast pants. A few minutes later, I heard someone pounding on my bedroom door. I started crying and crawled deeper under my bed.

"Come on, Kassey! Open the door!" I heard my brother's voices mutter and yell amongst themselves. I then heard the door break open and come off of its hinges as they came into the room. I didn't move from under the bed. I tried to make myself invisible as I saw the shoes of my

brothers walk around my room and stop in front of my bed. I held my breath for what seemed like forever. Zane's face then appeared in front of me and I let myself scream a scream of bloody murder. My brothers, Zane and Jasper, pulled me from under the bed and made me face them. Their eyes had a mischievous look, and I saw the anger underneath.

"You get what you give, Kassey." Jasper said mockingly.

I let out another scream—

The memory cut and went to another.

I heard a knock on my door and looked up from my book.

"Come in."

I saw my brother, Khalil, come into my room with slow, calculated steps. He seemed almost unsure or uneasy, and that made me worried. Was he ok?

"Khalil, what's wrong? Are you ok?" I set my book aside and stood up.

"I'm ok. Don't worry, sis. Amelia just took the kids out for ice cream and said she'll be back soon." He explained slowly.

"Oh, thanks. Um, is there something else?" He looked at me for a long time and that made it seem like that wasn't why he had come to see me.

Khalil came toward me until he was close enough that I could feel his breath on my face. He lifted a hand to move my hair behind my ear.

"Has anyone ever said that you had meticulous eyes?" He asked me as he placed his hand on my cheek.

Alarm bells went off in my head and I backed away from him, but I miscalculated how close I was to my bed, and I fell back onto my blankets. Khalil smiled at me and kept coming closer.

"Khalil, what are you doing?" I straightened myself up. I saw him climb onto my bed.

He ignored me and came close enough that he could reach out and touch me. My brother grabbed my arm and pulled me closer to him. I couldn't get out of his grip, no matter what I did.

"Khalil—" He kissed me, long and hard, until I slapped him with my free arm. He looked at me with a face full of hurt and I felt bad for a moment, but my mind screamed at me to not show him any sympathy. Khalil's hurt turned to anger. He pushed me down and undressed me. I screamed and kept telling him to stop, but he persisted to ignore me no matter how loud I screamed. I screamed for Amelia, but I then remembered that she wasn't there. It was only me and Khalil in the house, and that was what he wanted. Khalil had fully undressed me and persisted to kiss me as I cried for him to stop.

Khalil looked me in my eyes and smiled. He didn't seem to see the pain I was in or the fear that I felt. He seemed like he was enjoying my discomfort.

"Shh...it's alright, Kassey. Don't worry. Everything's going to be fine." He coaxed me.

I looked at him with as much hate as I could manage. "You will never get away with this, Khalil."

"Oh, honey...I already have."

"Kassey?" Evan was shaking me as I sat there frozen. Everyone at the table was staring at me. I blinked and looked over at my boyfriend. His face masked the same feeling I had seeing that last memory: Fear, worry, and helplessness. I got up from the table and ran out of the department.

I ran away from the building and to the street across from it. I stopped and leaned against a tree. It hurt to breathe; it hurt to run, it hurt to think. Everything inside of me hurt. I now realize that I was remembering nothing but the wonderful memories. My mind had pushed back all the unbearable things and made them seem like they didn't exist. That moment, when everything came forward at once, it took me over and overwhelmed me to where it was all I could think about. I couldn't push it away because it demanded to be known.

"Kassey!"

I looked up, even though I didn't want to, and saw Evan running toward me. I couldn't focus on him. I felt like I was coming apart from the seams. I couldn't breathe, I couldn't focus on anything, and my mind was going back and forth from one memory to another. Evan came up to me slowly, like he was trying to figure out what mood I was in. I could tell he was worried and I was glad that he had come after me.

"Are you ok?" He gently grabbed my face and looked into my eyes. Evan was always gentle with me and that was one reason I loved him. We hadn't exactly said that we loved each other yet, but we had that type of relationship where we didn't have to say the words, and we could still know how we felt towards each other. Just saying it would strengthen us more than we already were.

"I-I'm s-sorry.." I gasped.

"Don't worry. Can you breathe? You're shaking." Evan looked me over. "Kassey, tell me what's wrong. What do you need?"

"I remembered...I'll be fine." I counted in my head to calm myself down, but it wasn't working.

"Kassey, tell me the truth. How many fingers am I holding up?"

"This is s-stupid, E-Evan." I turned away from him.

"No, it's not. You're not speaking right. How many fingers?" His voice sounded stiff.

I tried answering him and he got more worried when I answered him wrong. Evan took my hand and ran us to his car, then he quickly drove me to his house. When we got there, he dragged me into the kitchen, where he made the place a complete wreck. He sat me in a chair at the table while he ran around the kitchen.

Evan's sister, Elena, ran into the kitchen. "Hermano, what are you doing?"

"¡Déjame en paz, hermana!" Evan yelled at her.

"Oh, Dios mío." Elena left, shaking her head.

"What are you looking for?" I spoke slowly. I had put my head down, but my eyes still tried to follow him as he ran rampant back and forth.

"Something. Don't talk." He went to the cabinets. "Found it!" He pulled out something I couldn't see. When he was finished, he came up to me with a cup and a pill.

I gave him a look, and he gave a little laugh. "I'm not trying to kill you. I promise. It's something my parents give me whenever I'm sick. The pill goes with the drink. It's like an herbal tea with medicine. It also helps with panic attacks." Evan explained.

I nodded and slowly lifted my head to take the pill with the drink Evan gave me. I didn't immediately feel better. Evan carried me to his room and let me lay on his bed for a few hours. When he left, I lay there staring at the ceiling. I could see my memories swirling together, playing multiple pictures and scenes back and forth.

"Kassey, this is Amelia. She's going to be taking care of you while you stay here."

My social worker, Ms. Reynolds, told me.

I stared at the woman for a while. She said hello to me and introduced me to everyone in the house.

"Kassey, these are your brothers, Khalil and Eric, and these are your sisters, Sarah and Jenna."

No one smiled at me, but I wasn't looking at them. I was looking at Khalil because his face was the only one that had a smile—

I screamed as Zane pulled me from under the bed and threw me onto the ground. I tried crawling away from them, but my brothers pulled me back by my legs and watched me with sick amusement as I kept trying to get away repeatedly.

"You get what you give, Kassey. Remember that!" Jasper pulled me up again and slapped me across my face. The force made me fall to the floor again, but I didn't get back up this time. Both brothers laughed at me—

"Get off of me!" I screamed at Khalil. I tried pushing him off of me, but he wasn't budging. He had a smile on his face and I've never hated that smile as much as I did now. Before, I always thought his smiles were full of warmth and love, but now I knew his smiles were cold and heartless.

Khalil's smiling face turned to annoyance, and he grabbed my neck as hard as he could. I clawed at his arm, but he didn't seem to notice. I gasped for air and kept calling his name, but he wouldn't let up. His grip never lessened, but my air depleted little by little until I passed out.

*   *   *   *

"Kassey!"

I jumped up from the bed, gasping for air. The last memory I had felt so real that, when I woke up, I felt like I wasn't getting enough air. I looked over at Evan's perturbed face and put my hand to my chest to slow my breathing. Thinking of Khalil and my brothers always gave me panic attacks and chills.

"Are you ok? You were screaming in your sleep." Evan told me.

"Yeah, I-I just...had a nightmare. I'm fine." I breathed. I didn't even realize I had fallen asleep.

Evan stared at me for a while until he just shrugged. "Um, Hayley called, and she's worried about you. She asked if you could come back to the house. Do you feel better?"

"Yeah, I'm—" I heard my phone ring. Evan got up to get it and gave it to me.

"Hello?"

"Kassey? Oh! I've been trying to reach you for so long! Are you ok?" I heard Hayley's voice on the other line and she sounded very concerned.

"I'm sorry. I didn't have my phone." I knew my voice lacked any emotion, and that seemed to make Hayley even more uneasy.

"Well, I want you to come back. Evan called and said you needed some time for yourself for a while, but I think you need to come back now." She said demandingly.

"Um, ok. I'll be there soon." I hung up the phone and groaned.

Evan tilted his head at me. "Are you ok?"

"N—Yes...I mean, no. I mean…" I stammered.

"Kassey, tell me the truth."

"I wasn't expecting to see them there. My father was so cold and my mother was so lost. They weren't the same people I grew up with. They seemed...broken down." A thought then went through my mind. "Did Samson ever text or call you?"

"No, why?"

"That would be the only way the police would know to come to the house for me. I saw him at the jail. Maybe they traced him somehow or something." I said my thoughts aloud. Evan's face turned to confusion, and I told him to just forget it. I had him drive me to the house, then gave him a quick kiss before I went inside.

The house was cold when I came in. As soon as I closed the door, Hayley found me and hugged me as hard as she could. I grunted, then stiffened, and she took that as a hint to step back.

"Are you ok? What happened? Tell me everything." She rambled.

"Slow down, ok? They asked me a few questions and then had me sit down and wait for someone." I slowly explained.

"Wait for who? Did they terrorize you?"

"No, they asked me straight questions. I deflected when I could. Nothing they said phased me, but they had me meet my parents." I watched her face for any type of emotion.

"W-What?" Hayley sounded stunned.

"Um, yeah. I didn't know they would do that. It didn't exactly go as I would've liked. Both my parents differed from how I remembered them."

"How different?"

"My dad was cold, while my mother was lost and troubled. They both spent a lot of time in prison and were broken down. They aren't the same. At all." I knew I sounded sad, and Hayley gave me another hug. This time I accepted it.

*　　*　　*　　*

For the next few days that turned into weeks, I visited my parents five times. Our relationship has improved and today, I was scheduled to meet them again. Last time I went, they said they would have some news for me, but they wouldn't tell me what. I was doing better in school and my relationship with Evan and my family has grown even stronger. I also have had no terrible encounters with anyone bad from my past. I was very grateful for that.

"Are you ready to go?" Hayley came into my room and asked me just as I finished getting dressed.

"I guess." I said, rolling my eyes.

Hayley came in and sat on my bed. "I thought you guys were getting along."

"We kinda are. My dad is still distant from me. My mom has gotten happier and we are getting along more." I leaned against my dresser and crossed my arms as I looked at Hayley.

"Who are you closer to?"

"My mom. My dad was a good parent, but we didn't do as much as me and my mom. We had a different bond. Me and my dad got along through sports and activities, while me and my mom got along by doing stupid things and her taking care of me when I was sick. The roles were different." I explained.

Hayley nodded. "So, you don't want to go?"

"I'll go. I want to see what they want to tell me." It has been on my mind ever since I saw them last. They seemed so happy, but hesitant when they told me. I wondered if I would be happy with whatever they had to tell me. Hayley helped me get some breakfast and drove me to the police department. I tried calling Evan, but he was asleep, so I left him multiple messages to get back to me. I really wanted to hear from him. I wanted him to tell me that everything was going to be ok. I didn't want to walk in blindfolded and unable to react to what they were going to say.

They had me wait in the cafeteria just like they did every time I came here. I didn't mind it. I got to look around and run a few thoughts through my head. After a few agonizing minutes, the doors opened, and I saw my parents come into the room with two police officers following them. My parents sat down and I saw my mother's bright smile. I could tell she wanted to give me a hug, but remembered the guard that observed us all. We were the only ones in the room. It was very early in the morning and none of the other inmates were even awake.

"I've been waiting to see you again, Kassey!" My mother said excitedly.

"I wanted to see you my whole life, mom. Both of you." I looked at my mom and then at my dad's distracted face.

Ash's face dropped. "Kassey, we're really sorry about that. Honestly."

"That's in the past. We need to focus on the future." My father chimed in.

"Right, so what did you want to tell me?"

"So, your father and I have been here for a few years and we have served our time. They were thinking of letting us out on good behavior and with 2 year probation." My mother explained.

"Two year probation?" I stared at them. That means they're getting out?

"Probation is—"

"I know what probation is, dad." I cut him off sharply.

He nodded to me, not taken aback by my tone. "We will have to tell them everywhere we go, and we can't go out of the state." My dad explained further.

"So, you're getting out." I didn't say it as a question, but my mother nodded as an answer.

"Yes, we are."

"When?"

"Tomorrow." They said it together. The word came out slowly and I could tell they were watching my face for a reaction. Tomorrow? That soon? I didn't know if I was happy or not. *Of course I'm happy. This is just all so sudden. How much will this change things?* My mind questioned the exact thing I was afraid of. My parent's release was a food thing, but I didn't know what would happen after that, and that was what scared me the most.

"Good. Ok, that's...good. I'm glad you guys are doing good." I knew my words sounded forced, but they seemed to take it.

"When we get out, we wanted you to live with us." My mother added.

"W-what?" I blinked at them.

"We want you to live with us, Kassey. You are our daughter and we want you to be with your family." My father said softly.

"I-I have a family." The words slipped out of my mouth before I could think.

I saw my mom's eyes glisten, but her voice didn't betray her face. "We know you have grown attached, but this would not be permanent. I meant it when I wrote that note and said we were going to come back for you. We want you to be with us now."

"I-I can't just leave them. I've been with them for at least a year. I like them. They actually care about me and we all act like a family. You can't just take me away from them." I was getting upset.

Neither of them said anything for a while. They both looked defeated, but my father spoke up first. "If you change your mind, let us know. We want you to be with us. We want to be a family like we once were." My dad got up and left us.

My mother reached across and rubbed her thumb against my hand. "We love you. Never forget that." She got up and followed her husband.

I watched them leave, but as their words swirled in my mind, I realized we would never be the family we once were.

CHAPTER TWENTY-FOUR

"They want you to do what?" Evan asked me after I told him everything that happened.

We were in his bedroom. His family had left for another vacation and Evan was home alone. I told him it was stupid that they kept doing that, but he didn't seem to care. His answer was, "I get the house to myself and I get to invite you over anytime."

"They want me to come live with them." My voice sounded sad.

"When are they getting out?"

"Tomorrow."

"Tomorrow?!" Evan's eyes bulged.

"Yeah, I was surprised, too. Part of me wants to go, but another part of me doesn't."

"¡diablos, no! They can't do that! That's not fair to you!" Evan yelled.

I got up from the bed and walked up to him. "You know I can't understand what you're saying sometimes when you talk in Spanish. You talk too fast, especially when you're mad." I put my hands on his shoulders to stop him from shaking.

"Sorry. It's just that—they can't just come in here and start changing things around. You just got settled with the Johnsons and everything's fine. Now, they want to uproot you and expect everyone to be fine with it? It's not fair, and it's selfish." Evan said angrily.

"I know, but they are my parents and I said that I wanted to find them and put our family back together. This would be me following through on that."

"Where were they when they promised to come back for you? Why didn't they do the right thing and stop what they were doing for you? For the safety of their daughter? That's the main reason their asses landed in jail!"

I sighed and sat back on the bed. Evan came over and sat next to me. He tilted his head at me and waited for me to get my thoughts together. "They couldn't come back for me because they got arrested. I'm not making excuses for them. They are still my parents, but I felt the distance between us."

"What do you want to do?"

"I want to give them another try. I kinda owe that to them. I want to hear their story."

I could tell Evan didn't agree with me, but he respected my decision. He could see that it still upset me, so Evan changed the conversation to something else. I was glad he was still here with me through all this craziness and willing to help me with the things I needed to understand.

"So, the guys wanted to officially meet you. Last time was kinda bad because they didn't want to make you upset in the hospital. If you're up to meeting them…" He trailed off while waiting for my answer.

"Yeah, anything would be better than worrying about my messed up life."

"Cool, because they will be here soon." Evan kissed my forehead and headed downstairs and into the kitchen.

I followed him. "What are you doing?"

"I am getting some food together because they are always hungry when they come. Also, I went looking for fresh food and I think I found something that you might like." He said while looking in the fridge.

"You bought me food?" Aww.

Evan smiled sheepishly at me. "Yeah, it's no big deal. I wanted you to have some food to eat. Do you want to try it?"

Evan gave me some crackers and Boortsog, and I laughed when I recognized the latter. I remembered when I went to the Mongolian grill and Evan ordered that for me when we ate lunch.

"I went back for some and Monte gave me some to go." He explained when I pointed it out.

"You really didn't have to get this for me. You already do a lot and spend a lot of money for me." I took another bite.

"Like I said, I don't mind." Evan shrugged.

"¡Eress el mejor!" I smiled at him.

Evan's face fell blank in his surprise. I choked on my food as I laughed. I had been studying a little more Spanish so I could talk to Evan's family and not feel stumped whenever they asked me something.

"When did you learn that?" He sounded breathless.

"I've been studying for a few weeks."

"Do you know what you said?" He still didn't seem like he believed I had said a correct sentence in Spanish.

"You're the best!" I responded cheerfully and messed up his hair.

"Alright. You learned some Spanish. That's great." He looked happy as he tried to fix his hair.

"I still don't know what you and your sister said the other day."

"It's alright. Not all of us can be know-it-alls." He joked.

I punched his shoulder. "Shut up!"

"Ow. You punch hard." Evan rubbed his shoulder.

"I'm sorry. Forgive me." I wrapped my arms around his neck and he put his hands on my waist and pulled me closer to him.

"I know how you can win back my respects." He spoke softly.

"Oh yeah? How?" I looked into his light eyes.

Evan kissed me, sweet and lingering, and I gracefully accepted his kiss. Evan was never hungry or needy. He simply gave you what you were comfortable with and never pushed you past your limits. He grabbed tighter onto my waist and lifted me onto the counter. He slowly pulled my shirt over my head and I worked on the zipper of his pants. Out of nowhere, as soon as I felt cold air rush at my skin, my mind screamed at me to stop. I didn't know what happened, but I suddenly lost my nerve. When my body tensed, Evan sensed my mood change and looked up at me.

"Are you ok?"

"I-I can't. I-I'm sorry. I just—"

"What's wrong?"

"It's not you, ok? I just...things have happened to me in the past that kinda have me scared and…" I trailed off as I tried to find the right word.

"Unsure?" He finished for me.

"Yeah. I'm sorry."

"Don't worry about it. I understand." He said he understood, but I could tell he was disappointed. I hated the fact that one person and one terrible memory could make me this unraveled after years have passed. Evan and I slowly dressed ourselves in silence, then Evan moved himself into the living room while I stayed in the kitchen. We filled the house with brutal silence. Just when I was thinking of going to talk to him, the doorbell rang. I heard the voices of Evan and his friends, but I made no move to greet them. I was still feeling the stupidity of me stopping while we were kissing. I did not know what was on Evan's mind, and even though he said he was fine, I didn't get that impression at all. I heard the guys come into the kitchen, but I made no move to react. They didn't seem to notice.

"Kassey, you remember the guys, right?" Evan asked me. When I risked looking at him, his head was turned to the side and he wasn't looking directly at me.

I sighed. "Yeah, I do. Hey guys." I knew my voice lacked any emotion.

His friends looked between Evan, and I like they could feel the tense atmosphere in the room. "You guys ok?" His friend, Aiden, asked.

"We're fine. Don't worry." Evan reassured them dismissively.

"Well, alright! Let's go do something fun!" Quinn rubbed his hands together readily. Now I know where Evan got that motion from.

"Where do you want to go?" Evan asked. His voice seemed like he was feeling better. He was looking at his friends with genuine curiosity.

"Well, we've always wanted to go to the basketball court, and we know you like playing basketball, Kassey." Aiden looked at me with a smile.

"As fun as that may be, I think I'll just leave." I quickly tried to leave the kitchen. I heard them follow me, but I wouldn't allow myself to stop.

"Kassey!" Evan grabbed my hand as I went outside.

"Get off me." I glared at him and he reluctantly let me go.

"Why are you leaving? You love basketball." Evan frowned.

"I thought you wouldn't care about me leaving." I crossed my arms.

"What are you talking about?" Realization showed on his face. "Is this about what happened before?"

I didn't answer him, and he took that as a yes. "Kassey, I'm sorry if I made you feel a certain type of way, but I always want you with me, especially when the guys are here."

"Thanks, but you guys have fun, ok?" I started backing away from him.

"Look, at least let me drive you. It's not fair for you to walk that far."

"Evan—"

"Please?" He looked at me with so much longing that I felt bad for acting out.

"I don't want you to leave your friends for me." I tried one more time to dissuade him.

"I don't think they'll mind. Please, Kassey." Evan grabbed my hand and looked directly into my eyes.

After a few uncomfortable seconds, I let him drive me back. I could tell he was still upset about me leaving, but he was happy about being able to drive me. Evan stopped the car in front of the house and killed the engine.

"I'm sorry." I said quietly.

He didn't look at me. "For what?"

"Being an ass. It wasn't fair for me to pull you from your friends, and all I did was turn a happy time into something depressing." I explained with a sigh.

"You made nothing depressing, Amor. I understand why you wanted to leave, though I wish you didn't feel that way. I know you would've had fun. I think I'm most to blame for that." Evan turned his head to give me a smile.

I shook my head but knew arguing would do no good. "Thank you for driving me home." I started getting out of the car.

"No problem...Kassey?" Evan's voice sounded hesitant.

"Hmm?" I turned back to him.

"Before you go in, just let me show you something. Please." He bit his lip.

"Ok…" I got back inside but was nervous. Where did he want to take me?

Evan found something in the back of his car and blindfolded me. The moment I lost my sight, I wanted to reconsider getting back into the car. The drive wasn't that long and Evan took off the blindfold as soon as the car stopped. When I opened my eyes, I saw he took us to the movies.

I looked at him in disbelief. "You took us here?"

"I had a feeling you haven't had bad popcorn in a while." Evan joked.

I rolled my eyes. He was right, though. I haven't been to the movies in a long time. I enjoyed the movies more than I enjoyed shopping. Going to the movies, you get to eat junk food and ruin your brain with bad pickup lines, so I let him take me inside. Evan already knew what we were seeing, and it was a movie I had never heard of. He said it was a drama and horror movie. He also mentioned that I had told him what I liked to watch, and he remembered ever since. When I started gravitating toward the snacks and drinks, Evan saw me and asked me what I wanted.

"Stop spending so much money on me." I told him.

"I don't mind. Tell me what you want and I'll get it for you."

Evan bought us a small buttered popcorn, four churros, an orange Icee, and two boxes of candies. When we got ourselves settled into the theater, Evan sighed.

"I wasn't sure if you would want to come here with me." Evan explained after I asked him if he was ok.

"Why would you think I wouldn't want to come?" I turned in my seat to look at him.

"The, uh, last moment we had together, I made it awkward. Plus, I knew you were upset, so I wanted to make you feel better." Evan shrugged at me.

"Evan, things were awkward, yes, but we are here now. I don't want to think about the past anymore. Maybe, in the future, we will handle things better." I told him as I tried tickling him.

We got shushed by some people as the movie came on. We both ate most of the candies during the movie. There was a lot of drama and horror, along with funny scenes. I could tell Evan wasn't paying much attention to the screen as I was. In the corner of my eye, I could see him watching me as I reacted to the movie. Nearing the end of the film, I caught him smiling at me.

"What?" I asked him.

"Nothing." He shook his head and laughed.

"I think I ate too much candy." I said as I leaned back in my chair.

Evan laughed harder, and I glared playfully at him. I was having fun, and we both knew it. When the movie ended, the movie theater cleared out, but Evan and I didn't move from our seats.

"You want to stay until they come to clean the seats?" Evan asked me as I sat with my eyes closed.

"I think I had a sugar crash." I drawled.

In between my slit eyes, I saw Evan shake his head in disapproval. "Do you need help?"

"I need more life." I muttered.

"I'll take that as a 'yes.'" Evan grabbed my hands and slowly pulled me up. I protested for a little while, but Evan ignored me. Eating that much sugar and food made me feel so sluggish and nauseous that I didn't want to move. Before we left the building, Evan took me to the bathroom and held my hair as I puked out my guts. When he was sure I was ok, he slowly lifted me up and put his hand on my forehead.

"Are you ok?"

"Why are you in the girls' bathroom?" I asked him slowly.

"That is a question that is invalid at the moment. Now, I think we had too much fun." Evan looked me over.

"I'm fine. I'm glad I came here with you." I closed my eyes.

"I'm glad, too, but I don't think you'll be able to walk out of here yourself." I felt myself being lifted off the floor and carried until I felt the air become colder when Evan brought us outside. I let Evan carry me into the car and drive to the house, where he then carried me up to my room.

"Is she alright?" I heard Hayley's voice as she followed us into my room.

"Yeah, we, uh, ate too much candy, and she got a stomach ache." I heard Evan's voice as he laid me on my bed. He pulled me under the blankets and kissed my forehead. "Get better alright, love?" He whispered to me.

I mumbled an answer to him and I vaguely saw him smile. He ruffled my hair, and I heard his and Hayley's footsteps move towards the door. I heard them talk amongst themselves in hushed voices and I tried to keep myself awake to listen to their conversation.

"Is she going to be ok?" Hayley whispered.

"Yeah, I think sleep will help her feel better." Evan whispered back. "Can you tell her to call me tomorrow morning before school?"

I didn't hear Hayley's response before my eyes closed and sent me to sleep.

CHAPTER TWENTY-FIVE

The sun was really bright as it shone through my window the next morning. I slowly sat up and groaned as I felt a headache. What happened? Slowly, my mind worked. I remembered Evan taking me home and us going to the movies...then me getting sick and him having to take me home. I then remembered that Evan had asked for me to call him when I woke up.

"Hello?" He sounded groggy and it took him a while to answer.

"Hey." I didn't know exactly what to say.

"W-what time is it?" I heard his bed shuffle as he moved.

"Um," I looked at my phone really quick, "It's 6 in the morning."

"¡Mierda! Thanks for waking me up! I got to go!" Evan said then hung up.

I sat there dumbfounded for a moment with my phone still to my ear. Ok? What was the point of calling if I was basically just going to be his alarm clock? I heard shuffling in the hallway and then a knock on my door.

"Come in."

Hayley opened my door and peeked her head in. "Are you up?"

"Yeah, I guess." My phone pinged, and I looked at the message of Evan asking if I wanted a ride to school.

"Are you feeling better?" Hayley asked as I answered Evan, saying yes to the ride.

"What do you mean?" I put down my phone.

"Evan brought you home and he said that you ate too much and got sick. I thought I would check on you after a bit of sleep."

"Yeah, I'm fine. Don't worry about me. Um, Evan's going to give me a ride to school, so you don't have to worry." I pushed past her and went to claim a bathroom.

Running down the stairs, dressed and ready, I quickly headed into the kitchen and tried to find something to eat. When I came up empty, I gave up and waited until Evan texted me to come outside.

"Kassey."

Jade came down the stairs and jumped onto the counter that was behind me. I leaned on the stovetop and crossed my arms so I could face her.

"What's up?"

"Can I talk to you about something?" Jade shifted uncomfortably.

"Talk to me about what?" I tilted my head.

"Hayley told us that your parents want you back."

"She did?" What did she tell them? "What did she say?"

"Hayley told us that your parents were in jail and they were getting out soon, but they wanted you to go with them when they got out." Jade explained.

"Yeah, that's pretty much it."

"Is that what you want?" Jade's face looked like she was expecting an answer she didn't want to hear.

"I want to because they are my parents and I want our family to be back together, but I don't because I haven't seen them in years and it'll be too hard to go back to how it was before." I didn't enjoy saying what I had been thinking for a while, but what I said was the truth. I was conflicted about going back with my parents.

"Well, whatever you want to do, I won't stop you...just know that we are your family, too. Plus, we won't hesitate to help when you still need us in the future. I promise you that." Jade was looking at the floor when she said this and I could see her cheeks blush a little.

I smiled to myself. "Thanks, kid." I walked up to her and messed up her hair.

Jade punched my shoulder and gave me a sheepish smile. "Don't mention it."

I heard a car horn and ran outside to meet Evan. He waited until I had closed the car door and put on my seatbelt to drive to the school.

"So, what was the deal with you hanging up?" I asked him as soon as he pulled onto the road.

"Sorry about that. I didn't know that I slept in and—I know that's a crappy apology, but I really didn't mean to hang up on you like that." He patted my leg since he couldn't exactly look at me.

"Mhm. You're lucky I love you." The words slipped out of my mouth before I could think about what I was saying. I still hadn't realized what I said, but Evan's lack of words made me realize I said something he wasn't expecting. I saw him slowly sit up in his seat and stare more intently at the road. We filled the entire ride to the school with silence.

When we got out of the car, Evan still hadn't said anything. I was feeling like I had messed up again. "Evan, I'm sorry."

He looked genuinely confused. "For what?"

"For saying 'I love you.'"

"Are you apologizing for that? I would never make you feel bad for telling me how you feel. We just hadn't said it because I didn't want you to feel like we were moving too fast. I was ecstatic when you said that, but I also wasn't expecting it." Evan explained. He sounded so happy that I left it alone.

*   *   *   *

Evan and I had so much fun in psychology class. We were to look into a brain (a fake one) and label what functions were from where and how they work together to control the body. I was completely lost and Evan had to help me with most of it, but we had fun overall. It was a race in the class to see who could finish labeling the brain first and we came in second to a group of girls named Hope and Grace. I didn't mind, but Evan was a competitive person, so he was mumbling the whole time.

"Like, what the hell? How did we come in *second*?"

"It's ok, Evan. It really doesn't matter." I told him again after he had been rambling for over three minutes. He rolled his eyes and crossed his arms, but finally let it go.

Evan walked me to my second class. When he left, I missed him immediately for two reasons: One, I wouldn't see him until lunchtime. Two, I saw that Brianna was in class today.

Instead of sitting in my normal seat, I went to the one I had to take last week. I didn't pay any proper attention to her during class, but I caught her glancing at me multiple times. When class ended, I packed my things and headed out of the classroom. I heard Brianna call my name, but I didn't turn around. I hurried out of the classroom and to my locker, then cursed under my breath when I saw her walking in my direction. What did she want?

"Kassey, can we talk?"

I didn't look at her. "What is there to talk about?"

"Look, I've been terrible to you and I'm sorry about that."

"Terrible? Brianna, you pushed me out of my chair in front of everyone and you posted our personal business online! People started texting and reaching out to me to ask if everything was ok or if I did something. You put me in a bad spot." I inculcated her.

"Look, I said I was sorry, and you never answered me or gave me a chan—"

"Now you're putting it on me?!" People were looking by now, but I paid them no mind.

"Oh, my god. Listen, I didn't mean to do all of that. You were ignoring me and Emily. You wouldn't talk to us." She tried to justify herself.

"You never really tried, Brianna! If you were an actual friend then you would've tried to talk to me to the point it would've become annoying. Neither of you did that!" I started yelling.

"Well, maybe if you stopped being such a bitch then maybe I would've tried harder." She shot at me. There were lots of people crowding around us by now.

"Well, maybe if you weren't such an attention whore then more people would want to be around you." I shot back.

I felt something strike me across my cheek, followed by the feeling of my head hitting something hard, and I then found myself on the floor. Everyone who was watching gasped loudly, some went wild. Some were recording and others were cheering, while some looked like they would have a heart attack. In my semi-cleared vision, I saw Brianna lean over me with a face of surprise, but she didn't move to help me up.

I slowly got myself up in a slouching position, but my head spun with any movement I made. I saw Brianna's head snap up and look behind me at something I couldn't see. I heard more commotion and someone grabbed my waist to pull me up from the ground. I protested until I saw who it was.

"What the hell is going on?!" Evan's voice rose to a dangerous level in his anger.

"Evan, stay out of it." Brianna sounded calm.

"Like hell I will. Who touched her?! I want to know!" He practically screamed.

"Evan, please calm down." I asked him quietly. I knew what his anger did to him. He never thought through anything and he did stupid things. I turned and saw that some people had backed away and some even went into their classrooms. Whatever Evan's face showed, it was bad enough to make people back away. I tried to get out of his grip, but that only made Evan grab onto me harder. I'm not even sure he even noticed, given that he wasn't really looking at me.

"Evan, let me go. That hurts." I said softly to him. I didn't want to say that out loud and make the situation worse. I knew he wasn't trying to hurt me, but I didn't appreciate the tight grip. He still didn't hear me and I turned my wrist and dug my nails into his skin. He let out a low hiss and let me go, glaring at me a little bit.

"Relax, man. It's not a big deal." One guy randomly commented.

"She deserved it, though." Another chimed in.

"What did you say?" Evan's voice got dangerously quiet.

"I mean, when it's a catfight with girls, one is bound to get slapped or something, right? Someone probably cheated." The second guy responded, shrugging, but facing Evan head on when he saw that his further comment made things worse.

In a blur, I saw chaos erupt when both boys charged at each other and the administration came to break them up.

"Evan, this will help nothing." I rubbed his arm.

"They hurt you, Kassey." He spoke through his teeth.

"None of them hurt me. Brianna and I argued and I think she slapped me and I hit my head. It's fine." I knew that was a dumb explanation and not as fine as I tried it to make it seem, but I really wanted him to calm down. I appreciated him always looking out for me, but his temper always flared the worst with me.

Evan put his hand on my cheek and I flinched as my skin burned from being hit before. Seeing me jump seemed to make Evan even more mad. The administration took Evan, me, Brianna, and the guy Evan fought with into the main office for us to be questioned together. It was a long questioning that involved arguing and harsh words until the principal sent us all home. Since I came with Evan, he had to drive both of us home.

Evan marched out of the building, cursing under his breath and growling. I could tell he was still heated, so I let him vent the whole ride. When we got to the house, Hayley was standing outside with her arms crossed. I suddenly didn't want to get out of the car.

"Do you want me to talk to her?" Evan asked. After his session of venting, he calmed down a little, but I could still see he was pissed.

"No, I think I need to talk to her by myself." I sighed.

Evan nodded and gave me a quick kiss before I got out of the car. I walked up to my foster mother and saw the disappointment on her face.

"Do you want to talk here or inside?"

"It doesn't matter." I couldn't make myself look directly into her face.

"What happened? I got a call from your school saying that they were going to send you home. What happened to your face? Did you get into a fight?" Hayley gently touched my face, and I quickly closed my eyes as my skin flared up. Hayley got the hint and lowered her hand.

"I fought with Brianna and she slapped me." I said as an overall.

"You have blood on your face. Were you bleeding?"

"I hit my head on a locker when I fell. Evan saw and got mad and started fighting with some boy that said I deserved what I got." My voice sounded slurred and my mind was wheeling.

"Maybe I should take you to a hospital." Hayley suggested.

"No, no more hospitals. If I have to see another white room, I'll scream." I was getting so tired of being pricked with needles and asked questions. I've come to a point that I'd rather suffer at home than be taken care of by someone professionally.

Hayley took me to the bathroom and cleaned up my face and the back of my head. After she patched up my face, she left the situation alone for a while. I knew she wanted to talk about it more, but she decided to talk about something else.

"I have something to tell you." Hayley and I were sitting on my bed, facing each other.

"What?"

"Your parents got out this morning when you left for school. They are living in an apartment that is a few hours from here, and it's outside of town. They wanted me to bring you over to them when you got out of school." Hayley explained.

"They want to see me?"

"Yes, do you want to go? Do you want to call Evan first?"

I scoffed. This woman knew me better than I thought she did. Evan was always on my mind, especially when it came to my parents. Today, though, was a day that I was genuinely worried about him.

I told Hayley that I would call him and then we would leave. The phone rang for a while until I believed he wouldn't pick up. Then I heard his groggy voice.

"Hello?"

"Hey."

I heard something squeak as he repositioned himself. "Hey, what are you doing?" He sounded more awake.

"Um, Hayley didn't chastise me, and she cleaned me up." I told him.

"You're ok, right?"

"Yeah...I think." I sighed.

"You think? What's wrong?" I heard him get worried, and I imagined a frown on his face.

"Hayley told me that my parents wanted to see me when I came home from school. She wants to know if I want to go see them."

He was quiet for a moment. "Do you want to?" He finally asked.

"I'm still torn. I want to see what they have to tell me, but I'm not rushing to give up what I have now. Hayley said they live outside of town." I added.

"Outside of town? You'll be a few hours away?" I heard the sadness in his voice and that made me feel terrible.

"I'm sorry." I saw Hayley poke her head into my door and motion to me in a way that said, "Hang up and let's go." I nodded to her and quickly asked Evan the question that has been swirling around in my mind. "Are you ok?"

There was a long pause. "Yeah, I'm fine. I'm sorry I acted dumb. You know how I get when I see you like that." He sighed.

"I'm fine, Evan. You get uncontrollable in your temper."

"I know. I'm sorry. As long as I know you're ok, then I'll stop being stupid." I imagined a smile on his face.

"Thanks. Look, I have to go." Hayley was glaring at me.

"Ok, just call or text me when you can, Ok?" His voice started sounding sleepy.

I giggled. "I will. You go to sleep."

"Yes, ma'am." We both hung up and I looked up at Hayley.

"Come on." Hayley took me outside to the car and we drove to the apartment.

*　　*　　*　　*

The apartment was pleasant for people who just got out of jail. I didn't know the neighborhood, which was named Borenwood apartments, or the town that was called Willendale in the state of Georgia. It was a few hours outside of Baytonwood. The apartments weren't too close together and the lawns were neatly cut. The smell of flowers and freshly cut grass filled the air as Hayley and I arrived in the complex. The apartments all looked the same, except that they were painted different colors than others. Hayley and I got out of the car and headed toward the building with the number "33" painted on the door in black paint.

Hayley knocked on the door and we waited until the door opened. My mother took one look at us and her face brightened.

"Oh, Kassey! You're here! Come in." She moved aside to let us in.

There wasn't anything real in the house that would give the walls and floor any personality. There was more carpet than wood and some papers skewed on the floor, but other than some boxes in the corners, the house was bare.

"We just got here and we don't really have any possessions with us right now, so the house is kinda...empty." My mother explained when she saw me looking around.

"Mhm." I said. I didn't really know what else to say.

"Um, where's your husband?" Hayley asked when we all fell silent.

"He's trying to straighten things upstairs. I'll go get him." Ash smiled at me, then headed up the stairwell.

Hayley turned to me. "So?"

"So, what?"

"What are you thinking? How do you feel?" She prompted.

"I think...there is no life here. They lost basically everything and I guess this is them trying to literally start over." I looked at the walls again.

"Do you think you could—do you want to be here? Live here with them?"

It took me a while to answer. Did I really want to or was I just trying to make myself be here to honor a promise I made to myself years ago? "I think I can try." I finally said.

Hayley nodded and tore her eyes away as footsteps marched down the stairs. I saw my father come down behind my mother. He didn't look at us at first until he was face-to-face with us. He lacked any potent emotion, but he showed me a smile, so I guess I could take that over anything else. It was a start.

"When did you two get here?" He asked us.

"Not too long ago. Um, pleasant house. When are you going to decorate?" Hayley tried to start a conversation.

"When we get most of our things back. I hope." My father answered.

"How long are you guys on probation?" I asked as I looked down at their legs. I saw a bracelet around their ankles that had a blinking light.

My mom saw what I was looking at. "We may leave the house, but we can't leave the state. We also have to call in to our probation officer when we want to go somewhere."

"Like where?" Hayley tilted her head.

"Um, her school, the house you took her to, the movies, the store. Pretty much everywhere we go." She explained.

"For two years?" I added.

"Yes, we do that every day for two years. After the two years are up, then we no longer have to do that." My father chimed in.

"What if you don't let them know?" I already knew the answer, but I just wanted to hear what his answer was.

"Then we go back to jail." His answer was what I was expecting.

"So, you want me to stay here? With both of you?"

"Yes, Kassey. We would like for you to be here with us. I've always wanted to get you back so we can put our family back together. Please say you will come live with us." My mother said hopefully.

Everyone looked at me. I kept my face neutral. "How long would I be staying?"

"However long you would want."

"We are hoping you will stay with us for a long time. We are a family and you belong with us." My mom added.

"How about, she lives with you for a few months, maybe two or three, and from there, we see if she wants to stay or do something else." Hayley suggested.

"Is that what you want?" My mother asked me.

I nodded and that seemed to make everyone feel content. We settled the living arrangements. I will live with my parents for three months starting this weekend. That gave me two days to stay in Baytonwood with the Johnsons and Evan. I texted Evan and told him I was coming back into town. He texted me back and told me he was at the basketball court with his friends, so I had Hayley drop me off at the park. The ride to town was quiet and fast. Hayley asked me if I was happy with the living arrangement, but I couldn't find the words to answer her. After a few attempts at conversation, and me being quiet, she gave up.

After Hayley dropped me off at the park, I let myself take a brief detour before finding Evan. The last time I had been to a park was when I was 11 and living with my foster mother, Kesha, and my siblings, Victoria, Dan, and Ramone. They were the good family they placed me with, besides Alice. I don't exactly remember what happened for them to move me, but I remember being cared for and loved when I was with them.

"Come on, Kassey. We didn't come to the park for you to sit around and mope." My foster mother, Kesha, told me.

"Will you please stop?" I looked up from my phone and gave her an annoyed look.

She ignored my look. Kesha came up to me and pulled at my arms. "Kassey, just once. Please?"

"Will you just do it already, so she stops begging?" My older sister, Victoria, asked me as she looked at us from playing frisbee with my younger brother, Dan.

"Fine. If I do, will you promise to leave me alone?" I asked her.

My foster mother nodded, and I stood up, sighing, as I put my phone in my back pocket. Kesha smiled at me and spun around me as she danced in little circles. I slowly joined her, and soon, we were both dancing around and singing. Victoria pulled out her phone and played songs from her playlist, and Kesha had my siblings dance with us.

People started looking, but we didn't care. We were a small family, dancing together and doing what we love the most. When we left, I realized that I hadn't picked up my phone since we got into the car.

I jumped as I felt a hand on my shoulder. I spun around and saw Evan quickly move back, like I was going to attack him.

"Woah! Jumpy much?" He frowned at me.

"Sorry. I didn't know you were there."

"Lost in thought?" He guessed.

"Lost in the past." I muttered.

"You said you had something to tell me?" Evan shifted the basketball he was holding.

I looked him over. "I didn't realize how cute you looked until now."

He chuckled. "Thanks, but you're deflecting. What's going on?"

I sighed. I was deflecting. I knew he wouldn't like me being so far away for three months or more. "My parents live in the Borenwood apartments. Their new apartment is in Willendale, Georgia." I started.

"Willendale? That's two hours outside of town." He was already getting sad.

"Yeah, um, the apartment complex is nice, and it was quiet when we got there and when we left. The inside is kinda bare and everything, but they are hoping to get their things back." I explained to him.

"So, you like it?"

"It will be a change of scenery, but I want to see how this will go." I think I was saying this more to convince myself that I will enjoy being with them for so long.

He nodded. "What else?"

"They have ankle bracelets that they have to wear and they have to alert their probation officer of their whereabouts for two years." I added.

"How long are you staying?" Evan started dribbling the basketball he was holding. I guess he was fidgeting.

"Three months to see how I feel about everything. After that, I may or may not go back to living here." I talked slowly as I watched Evan's face. I could tell he was not happy about any of this.

"So, when are you leaving?" His voice had gotten quieter.

"This weekend."

He scoffed. "So, you only get two days at a normal life until you have to leave everything behind?"

"I guess so. Look, I'm not thrilled to do this, but I will not be that far away. I'm sure I'll still be going to school here and I'll come back whenever." I said, sounding confident.

Evan shook his head. "No, you won't. Kassey, Willendale is outside of town in a *completely* different town. They have different schools, different stores, and maybe a different district.

It was quiet for a minute. "So, what now?"

"Well, we just make the most out of the two days you have." Evan took my hand and had me play basketball with him and his friends for the rest of the afternoon.

*   *   *   *

For the next two days, everyone tried to make sure I had fun. Hayley took us all bowling, she took us back to the amusement park, and she even let us skip school one day to hang out together. Evan tagged along with us a few times until his family came back and he had to stay home. We called and texted each other all day and all night until we both fell asleep. It was fun to hang out with them, but it was also sad because we were all trying to cram in a week's worth of fun during my two-day period before I had to leave. I could tell everyone was upset about me leaving, but we all made the most out of the time we spent together.

When I was in my room, Jade and Aliyah knocked on my door. They moved with a pace that showed that they were on a mission. I put my book aside and sat up as I watched them march into my room.

"What's up, guys?"

"You are not leaving!" Aliyah yelled.

"Aliyah—"

"It's not fair, Kassey." Jade backed her up.

"Not fair to who?" I crossed my arms.

"You! They can't just come and take you away from us because they want to suddenly put the family back together. You got yourself settled here and you like living with us, right?" Jade asked me.

"Yeah, I do."

"Then, tell them you don't want to leave and that you already found your home." Aliyah said sternly.

I sighed. "I can't. As much as things may seem unfair right now, they were my parents first. Also, everyone here knew that I wouldn't be here permanently." I got up from my bed and walked up to them.

Aliyah looked at me with sad eyes. "You don't want to stay with us?"

I frowned at her. "I will always want to stay with you, and if things were different, moving wouldn't be on my mind. I was here because I didn't have a family of my own. Now that my parents are back, I have to go back to them."

Aliyah's eyes glistened, and she looked down at the floor. Jade shook her head. "This isn't fair." She mumbled.

"I know." Before I came here, leaving was always on my mind. I never really wanted to be here. I always wanted to find my parents and go back to living with them and being the big and happy family we always were. Now, Hayley showed me what family love looked like and how you didn't have to be with blood to feel cared for and loved. They showed me what I had been missing and what I forgot about when I moved from home to home. Now that I found it, I was being moved again and would have to rebuild my life in a completely different place that I didn't know...with people I didn't really know.

Jade and Aliyah left my room, and they left me alone with the thoughts that swirled around in my head. There was a question that was always lingering in my mind, unanswered and unacknowledged.

You've always wanted to be with your family, right? Now you have to decide. Which family do you really want?

CHAPTER TWENTY-SIX

I woke up to the sound of footsteps running rampant. It was still dark outside, but I knew I wouldn't be able to go back to sleep without knowing where the sound was coming from. I looked for my doll and went out of my room to see what was making the noise. I walked to my parents' room and saw that they cracked their door open. I slowly pushed the door open and saw that my parents were running back and forth to each corner of their room.

I looked at my mother as she quickly packed up their things. I watched as she and dad worked hastily. They seemed almost afraid. They left nothing behind in the places they rummaged through. I turned in circles as I watched them with a deep fascination. Why were they moving so fast? What was going on?

My mother looked at me and stopped packing. She kneeled down to my height and gently grabbed my shoulders and looked me straight in the eye. "Honey, we have to go now."

"Where are we going?" I asked softly.

"I can't say. We are going somewhere far away from here, but you can't come." My mother said sadly.

"Why not, mommy?"

"Just…where we are going, you cannot come. It's too dangerous to take you with us…you have to stay here. We will make sure you have a wonderful family that will take care of you. I promise we will come back someday."

I felt tears in my eyes. I didn't really understand, but I had a bad feeling that was gnawing at my stomach. I could feel that I would never see them again. My mother was saying goodbye. She had promised me they would come back, but I didn't know how long it would take for that day to come.

My mom kissed my cheek and stood up. She walked over to my dad and he quickly took their bags. My father stopped and gave me a quick hug and kiss, then stepped out the door. My mother went to follow him, but turned back to me. She looked at me sadly and mouthed, "I love you." She blew me a kiss, and I saw her eyes glisten with tears. As she walked out, my entire world exploded with light—

I slowly opened my eyes and saw multiple blurred figures crowded around me. I slowly moved my arms and saw that there were tubes that came out of them and connected to the surrounding machines. I felt too drowsy to move my head or any of my limbs too much. I saw the doctors rush towards me, felt the needle prick me further as they injected more medicine into my body, and then the world disappeared.

*   *   *   *

Today is the day I have to leave. When I woke up, I had a feeling of dread. Hayley told me I had until the afternoon, around dinnertime, until my social worker would pick me up and take me to the apartment. Before I went to bed last night, Evan and I talked until one in the morning. I was really close to falling asleep, but Evan made me promise I would call him in the morning.

So, now, that is what I am doing. Picking up my phone at ten in the morning to call my very overprotective, but lovable boyfriend. I loved the word when I thought about it and said it out loud. It just warmed my heart and made me feel so loved at the thought of him feeling that way about me.

"Hello, hello, hello! How's my beautiful girl doing today?" I heard his cheerful voice after the second ring.

"How much did you drink?" I asked him, giggling. I knew Evan to be a day drinker sometimes.

"I drink zero percent. I am happy to hear your voice! Plus, my parents would never let me drink in the house." His voice sounded bummed when he finished talking.

"You said you had something planned for me today. What were you thinking of doing?"

"That is for me to know…"

"And for you to never figure out." We finished together and laughed.

Evan told me to get dressed and he would pick me up in ten minutes. I took a five-minute shower and got dressed in red-brown capris and my blue cropped mini top Evan told me he likes. I kept my hair down because, last time I tried putting my hair in a ponytail, Evan took it out and said I didn't need to be so extra as to change my hairstyle, so I always kept my hair down. Plus, I liked it that way, too. When I went downstairs, everyone was up. They gave me smiles and hellos when I looked at them, but the morning was kind of low-key.

"We kinda did something for you and I hope it won't make you feel uncomfortable." Jason said as he came up to me in the living room.

"What do you mean?" I asked him as I bit into a piece of toast I stole from Cameron.

"We—well, Hayley found some more pictures of you and your family and put them together with some videos we made of your time here. She also found other videos when you were in other homes and added those. She wanted to have a little collage of your life to look at." He explained sheepishly.

I paused as I was mid-chew. She went through my life to put together a video of my life? How does that even make sense? How does this woman have any time to do any of the things she does?

"Um, I guess I have no say in this?"

"Nope, you don't." Hayley said singsongy as she walked into the room.

I rolled my eyes and knew that I was in for something. During breakfast, we all sat together in the living room and watched a video of my life. We sat through my happy and sad moments, along with pretty embarrassing and morbid moments. I was covering my eyes by the time it was over. Everyone started laughing, but I looked over at Hayley and saw that she had tears in her eyes. I slowly lowered my hands and tilted my head at her.

"What's wrong?" I whispered so I wouldn't alarm the other kids.

"You hid so much from me for a long time. Seeing your life like that...I know it felt weird to play what you went through right in front of you for others to see." She sniffled.

She was right, though. It was weird to literally have my life on display, but, right now, I didn't mind it. I trusted them and they trusted me. I felt close enough to them to show the little details of my past as they helped me try to deal with the horrors of my past life. I owed it to them to show that I would not hide from them anymore.

"It feels weird, but I know you guys understand, so I'm not ashamed. Not like I would normally be when I first came here." I answered her truthfully.

Hayley smiled and hugged me for a moment before letting go. When the doorbell rang, Cameron got up to let Evan inside. Evan followed my brother into the livingroom and he smiled when he saw me.

"Good morning, Mrs. Johnson." Evan said to Hayley.

"Good morning, Evan. Where are you two going?" Hayley turned to face Evan and got right to the point.

He gave a little laugh. "I have a few things planned for today. I just want her to have fun."

"Well, have fun." Jason said as he tried to find a good channel on the tv.

"Not too much fun." Jade and Aliyah said in unison.

I glared at them, but Evan just laughed. "You don't have to worry, little ones. I'll take care of her." Evan took me outside, but before I could head toward the car, he grabbed my hand to pull me back.

"What's wrong? I thought there was somewhere you wanted to go." I asked him, confused.

Evan took both of my hands and pulled me close to him. "I want to do something first." He said before kissing me.

When he broke it off, I was at a loss for words for a bit. "What was that for?" I asked him when my brain unscrambled.

"For you being you. I never really imagined myself here, you know, with you. Us, together. I like it. Now, I'm really glad I didn't ask my parents to go with them on that vacation." He chuckled.

I smiled. "Me, too. I'm glad you stayed."

"Speaking of staying, my parents know you're leaving and they want to see you. Is that ok or do you want to do something else?"

"You know I like your family. I don't mind going over there." I loved talking to his family, even though I don't exactly understand what they are saying. Something about them made them lovable and easy for me to be around them.

*   *   *   *

Evan drove us to his house, and his family met us at the front door. I guess they were waiting for me to come.

"Hola, Kassey! ¿Cómo estás?" His sister, Elena, asked me when we came in.

"Bien. Gracias. How are you guys?" I asked them. Evan's parents were in the kitchen, and his siblings were in the living room with us. Elena was sitting on the couch, while Evan's brother, Nicholás, was standing behind the couch with his arms crossed.

"We are fine, but we wanted to talk to you." His sister said.

"About what?"

"Evàn told us you were moving away to live with your parents. Is that true?" His brother spoke up.

"Um, yeah, it is. They want me to stay with them for at least three months and see how I feel about it." I told them.

"So it's a um…" Elena struggled for the word.

"Experiment?" Evan finished for her.

She and I nodded. "We'll see how this goes."

"How much will change when you leave?" Nicholás asked in a harsh tone.

"What is that supposed to mean?"

"You'll be too far away for Evàn to have anything to do with you. You'll run him around trying to stay with you while you're sitting there babysitting your jailmated parents." His voice didn't waver at all, but his words struck me silent. Where was all of this hostility coming from?

"¡Dios! Eres un hijo de puta! Why don't you leave her alone? It's really none of your business, Nicholás!" Evan yelled.

"¡Oh, Dios mío! Will you two stop acting like children?" Elena hissed at them.

"Nick, I know I will be farther away from Evan, but I won't stop trying to see him. That's not who I am. If Evan wants to keep trying to make this work, then I will, too. Distance or not." My tone was more forceful than I would've thought it would be. I guess I was glad for that because Evan's brother shifted a little, but didn't change his expression. I believe I got through to him a bit.

After the fight with Evan and his brother, everything went more smoothly. Evan's parents, Isabella and Isaac, came into the room and we talked for a little while. They wanted to say how they were sad that I had to move away, but to not be a stranger. I was always welcome in their home whenever I wanted. Evan pulled me out of the house and we went for a walk. There wasn't a lot he wanted to do, but the whole thing with his brother took a lot of the time he wanted us to spend together, so he thought taking a walk would give us time together.

"I'm sorry about my brother. I don't know why he acted like that." Evan said when we were a block away from his house.

"It's not alright, but I can understand where it came from. He was just looking out for his little brother."

"It still doesn't excuse what he said to you. He could've kept his mouth shut." He grumbled.

I stopped and waited until he realized I wasn't following him anymore. "What's wrong?" He asked me as he walked back to where I was.

"Your brother appears to be an...aggressive person, but what he said was right. Things will be harder and I will have to focus more on adjusting than anything else." It hurt me to think about how much this will change some things, but Evan's brother was right. Evan may want to make this work, and I will be happy about that, but we will have to go the extra mile to deal with the changes, and I don't know how that will work.

Evan thought for a minute before he answered. "You're right. It's not really that long of a distance, is it?"

"It's two hours from this town and it's in a whole other district. It's kinda a long way from here." I told him as I crossed my arms.

Evan came up to me and took my hand, which forced me to lower my arms. "Don't worry, alright? We'll figure this out. I promise." Evan closed his hands over mine and kissed them. "Stop worrying. You'll get wrinkles."

I laughed when I heard him reference what I had told him before when he was worrying. I told him that worrying would give him wrinkles. I'm not surprised that he used my past words against me. Evan and I walked a few blocks away from his house and back, then he drove me back home. I only had half an hour before Ms. Reynolds had to come and get me, so we all hung around the house for the remaining time. I finally showed Evan my room, and he kept bouncing up and down on my bed.

"Your sister was right. You act like a child." I said as I stood watching him mess up my bed.

"I don't care. Your bed is comfortable. Come here." He sat down and patted the space next to him.

I went and sat next to him, leaning in his lap. He wrapped his arms around my shoulders and we sat there rocking back and forth for a while. "I'm going to miss you." He suddenly said.

"Stop. Don't. I don't want to talk about that right now. Right now, it's just you and me. Here together. I don't want to talk about anything upsetting or complicated." I quickly cut him off.

He nodded. "You're right. Sorry, I won't mention anything depressing again." He kissed me repeatedly on my cheeks, forehead, and neck. I giggled as he ticked me and whispered in my ear. I'm glad he was here with me right now, so I wasn't alone. I've been alone for a while and I didn't notice how socially out of touch I was until now. Moving here actually was the best thing that had happened to me.

Evan held my hand as we walked downstairs. I held my bag against my shoulder and slowly met the crowd of people that stood at the end of the stairwell. They all looked up when they heard us come down. Time seemed to slow down as I looked ahead of everyone and saw the only person who really mattered. My social worker stood in the open doorway with a frown on her face. When our eyes met, I saw the sadness in them.

I reached the bottom of the stairs and I walked up to Ms. Reynolds with Evan standing by my side. She straightened her back and looked directly into my eyes, and I did the same. Before,

Ms. Reynolds made me feel like I was her responsibility. Now I saw her as someone who was just doing their job of putting people where they were needed.

"Are you ready?" The woman asked me.

"Can I have a minute before we leave?" I asked her.

Ms. Reynolds nodded to me and I turned to everyone behind me. Hayley was the first who came up to me for a hug. Evan let my hand go as she hugged me tight. She pulled back, but kept her hands on my shoulders. Hayley looked into my eyes. I could tell she was trying hard not to cry.

"Through all the hell you put us through, we still love you." Was the only thing she said.

I laughed. "You're right. I was a badass when I came here and I created a lot of storms, but I really enjoyed being here with you guys. I promise you that."

"What about me?" Cameron asked.

I rolled my eyes and went to give him a hug. "We both created a lot of storms together."

"Thanks?" He asked sarcastically.

I went to Jason and gave him a hug. "I thought you weren't the warm and fuzzy type?" He joked.

"I'm not, so take advantage while you can."

He shook his head. I moved on to where the girls were standing and Aliyah immediately ran toward me. I picked her up and smiled at her. She didn't smile back.

"I don't want you to leave. It's not fair." She said in a small voice.

"I know, Aliyah, but this is how things have to be. I'll still come to see you, ok?" I caressed her head. She still didn't look happy, but she didn't complain anymore. I put Aliyah down and walked over to the door where Evan was. He looked like he was losing the best thing in the world. I took his hands but couldn't look him in the eyes. I couldn't look at his face. I knew that if I did, I would become weak and question everything I was doing more than I already was.

"I will miss you." He said.

"We don't have to say anything. I just want to be here with you right now." I whispered as I played with his hands.

Evan lifted my chin with his finger to make me look at him. "I will always be there with you. I don't care if we are two hours apart or two minutes, I will always find a way to be with you so you no longer suffer in silence. That is how much *I* love *you*." His thumb rubbed my jaw, and he leaned in to kiss me. I was stuck on the part where he said he loved me. I was thrilled to hear him say that he felt the same way I felt. I pulled him closer to me and deepened the kiss. I never wanted to let him go. I blocked out the world around me until it was me and my boyfriend. I wanted to inhale his scent of bliss and nature. I wanted the smell to imprint inside my brain so that it was something I could have forever.

I had to let go of him when Ms. Reynolds told me it was time to get going. My hand slowly left Evan's, and I saw his face drop as he moved to go stand with everyone else. I followed the woman to the door but didn't follow her outside, not yet. I turned to face everyone

one last time to imprint their faces into my memory as well. When I knew it was time, I followed

Ms. Reynolds out the door and never looked back at the house again.

They would be missed, but they would never be forgotten.

CITATIONS

Mooradia, G., Morgan, M., Godfrey, W., & Rosenberg, M. (2008). Twilight [Film]. United

States; Summit Distribution.

(n.d.). Retrieved May 12, 2019, from

https://www.google.com/search?rlz=1CACVLN_enUS837&ei=jW0vXvmpGvWEytMPk4qSgA

c&q=english+to+spanish&oq=english+to+&gs_l=psy-

ab.1.0.0i131i67l3j0i67j0i131i67j0l5.14062.15530..17382...0.1..0.189.1322.2j9......0....1..gws-

wiz.......0i71j0i273j0i131.OZMXElCGGh0&safe=active&ssui=on

(n.d.). Retrieved July 6, 2019, from https://www.google.com/maps/dir/Georgia/Tybee

Island, Georgia31328/@32.1553337,-

82.9983953,8z/data=!3m1!4b1!4m14!4m13!1m5!1m1!1s0x88f136c51d5f8157:0x6684bc10ec4f

10e7!2m2!1d-

82.9000751!2d32.1656221!1m5!1m1!1s0x88fb7f73b7a88301:0x4207db76949a9818!2m2!1d-

80.845666!2d32.0002152!3e0

Stephen F. Austin State College Athletics. (n.d.). Retrieved September 10, 2019,

from https://sfajacks.com/sports/mens-basketball/roster/shannon-bogues/2189

Shannon Bogues. (n.d.). Retrieved May 10, 2019, from

https://gleague.nba.com/player/shannon-bogues/

Aacap. (n.d.). Retrieved May 10, 2019, from

https://www.aacap.org/AACAP/Families_and_Youth/Facts_for_Families/FFF-Guide/Foster-

Care-064.aspx

Pregnancy, Parenting, Lifestyle, Beauty: Tips & Advice. (n.d.). Retrieved January

2, 2019, from https://mom.com/kids/5866-how-can-foster-care-affect-mind-child/

Hemispheres: Left & Right Hemispheres Roles, Facts & Information. (2019,

September 26). Retrieved May 12, 2018, from https://brainmadesimple.com/left-and-

right-hemispheres/

Rettner, R. (2014, March 28). Heart of the Matter: 7 Things to Know About Your

Ticker. Retrieved July 18, 2018, from https://www.livescience.com/44460-heart-

facts.html